Mary Anne vs. Logan

**Other books by
Ann M. Martin**

Ma and Pa Dracula
Yours Turly, Shirley
Ten Kids, No Pets
Slam Book
Just a Summer Romance
Missing Since Monday
With You and Without You
Me and Katie (the Pest)
Stage Fright
Inside Out
Bummer Summer

BABY-SITTERS LITTLE SISTER series
THE BABY-SITTERS CLUB series
(see back of the book for a complete listing)

Mary Anne vs. Logan
Ann M. Martin

AN
APPLE
PAPERBACK

SCHOLASTIC INC.
New York Toronto London Auckland Sydney

Cover art by Hodges Soileau

ISBN 0-590-43570-1

12 11 10 9 8 7 6 5 4 3 2 1   1 2 3 4 5 6/9

Printed in the U.S.A.   40

First Scholastic printing, February 1991

*This book
is in honor
of the birth of
Olivia Connett Swomley*

Mary Anne vs. Logan

CHAPTER 1

"How do I look?" I asked.

"Look? You look just fine," replied Dawn. "Anyway, you're only going to baby-sit for Jenny. What's the big deal?"

"I don't know. I guess Mrs. Prezzioso is the big deal. You know how she's always dressed. And how she always dresses Jenny."

"Yeah. They look like contestants in a mother-daughter beauty pageant."

Dawn and I giggled. Dawn is not only one of my two best friends; she's my stepsister. It was a Friday night and I was getting ready to sit for Jenny. Dawn was perched on a chair in my room.

"You know what?" I went on. "Mrs. P. has only gotten worse since she found out she's going to have another baby."

"I can't believe that *we* know what the baby is going to be, and the rest of the BSC members don't. They don't even *want* to know, Mary Anne."

"They want to be surprised, that's all," I said.

(BSC stands for the Baby-sitters Club. Dawn and I and a bunch of our friends belong to it. I'll tell you about it later.)

Who am I? I'm Mary Anne Spier. I live in an old (*very* old) farmhouse with Dawn, my father, and Dawn's mother. In case you're wondering, Dawn and I have been friends longer than we've been stepsisters. After our parents got married, Dad and I and my kitten, Tigger, moved into Dawn's house. That's because it's bigger than my old house was. Since we're pretty new at being a family, I call Dawn's mother Sharon, and Dawn calls my father Richard. That feels more comfortable than Mom and Dad. All things considered, our family is coming together pretty well. We have our tough times (what family doesn't?), but the good times are getting to be more frequent, and they last longer.

Let's see. I have brown hair, brown eyes, and a boyfriend! His name is Logan Bruno. Sometimes it's hard for me to believe I have a boyfriend. That's for two reasons: 1. I'm really shy. I bet I'm the shyest eighth-grader at Stoneybrook Middle School. 2. For awhile now, Logan and I haven't been getting along all that well. We've hit a few rough patches. There was the time when Dawn, Claudia (another BSC member), and four kids went on a sailing trip and got stranded on a little island off the coast. (It's a long story.) Practically everyone here in Stoneybrook, Connecticut, was looking for them or worrying about them. (I was a worrier. I wanted to be a searcher, but I have very fair skin, so I can't stay out in the sun too long.) Anyway, right before the sailing accident, Logan and I had a fight. It was a big one, but it was over the smallest thing. I learned something from that fight. I learned that Logan and I don't always trust each other. And I learned that Logan can't always be counted on in a crisis. He wasn't there when I needed him the most. I thought he could put our fight aside while our friends were lost at sea. But he couldn't, or didn't, until just before the end of the crisis.

We did make up after that, but it hasn't been our only fight. We had a pretty good one during another crisis — when Tigger was missing. Tigger is *little!* He's just a bundle of soft, gray, tiger-striped fur and a lot of purrs. He could have been in big trouble (although it turned out he wasn't). So while he was missing, I was scared to death — and Logan and I weren't getting along.

Logan and I have had some other difficult times, too. This is hard to believe, since everything was so great when we first met and realized we liked each other. For one thing, I couldn't fathom that a boy even liked me. I was shy, mousy Mary Anne. And Logan was this drop-dead handsome guy. He looks exactly like my favorite star, Cam Geary. Plus, he's from Louisville, Kentucky, and he has a wonderful Southern drawl. Everyone loves the way he sounds. Yet Logan chose *me* for his girlfriend. We've given each other gifts, gone to school dances together, and been out on dates. Plus, Logan was with me the day I chose Tigger at the animal shelter.

So Logan and I started off with a great relationship. But lately he's been a little pushy. At least, that's the way it seems to me. Sometimes I wonder if I'm falling *out* of love with Logan, but I don't think so. Not over a few tiffs and misunderstandings.

"So, anyway," I said to my stepsister, "do I look nice enough for Her Highness?"

"Like a real princess," Dawn answered, even though I was just wearing jeans and a new baggy sweater. "Go find your crown and you'll be all set."

I laughed. Then I checked my watch. "I better get going," I said. "I'm supposed to be there in twenty minutes."

The phone rang then, and Dawn said, "I'll get it. You find your crown."

I was looking for my shoes when Dawn called, "Mary Anne! It's for you!"

"Okay!" I called back. I dashed into our parents' bedroom, where Dawn was standing, holding the phone out to me. "Thanks," I told her. I took the receiver, and Dawn immediately left the room. That was a sure sign that Logan was on the other end of the line. If any of our other friends had called, Dawn would have hung around to see what was going on. But she respects my privacy where Logan and I are concerned.

"Hello?" I said.

Sure enough, the voice that returned my hello belonged to Logan. "Hi, it's me."

"Oh, hi," I said. "I can only talk for a couple of minutes. I'm on my way to the Prezziosos' to sit for Jenny."

"Can I talk you into going to a movie instead?"

"Right now? No. I really can't." I hated to

disappoint Logan, but I had a responsibility as a baby-sitter.

"Aw, come on. You and I are a couple, Mary Anne," said Logan.

"I know we're a couple," I replied, "but . . . um . . ." I tried to explain what I was thinking. I couldn't. I have a little trouble expressing myself. And when I do show that I'm angry or upset, I usually start to cry — which was not going to help this situation.

When I didn't finish my sentence, Logan said, "Well, is Dawn free to sit tonight?"

"You mean, to take over at the Prezziosos' so I can go out with you?"

"Yeah."

"Logan, I can't send Dawn on my sitting job," I said, my voice trembling.

"You mean you won't come to the movies with me?" Logan sounded confused.

"Well . . . no."

"Okay," said Logan uncertainly.

"I have to go," I said in a rush. "I'm about to be late. I'll talk to you tomorrow."

We hung up the phone then, and I had to force myself not to cry. I concentrated on Jenny. That was my job. I could think about Logan some other time.

I left the house in a hurry then, and ran all the way to the Prezziosos'. (They live nearby, and it was still light out.) I made it just in time.

Mr. and Mrs. P. left pretty quickly, so soon I was alone with Jenny. When her parents had left, Jenny held out her wrist and said, "Look. Mommy bought me a watch! I can't tell time yet, but a watch is a very grown-up thing to have. That's what Mommy said. She bought me some other stuff, too. Want to see?"

"Sure," I replied.

I followed Jenny upstairs to her bedroom. Jenny, as usual, was dressed to the nines. That's what my friend Kristy's stepfather would say, meaning that Jenny was very dressed up (even though it was just a regular old day). Mrs. P. *loves* to dress up Jenny and herself. That's what Dawn meant when she said they look like contestants in a mother-daughter beauty contest. They look like that most of the time.

Jenny took my hand and pulled me into her room. "Here," she said, heading for her dresser. "Mommy got me more grown-up stuff. Stick-on earrings, and look — sneakers with *laces*. Mommy says big girls learn how to tie their shoes."

"Wow, that's great, Jenny!" I exclaimed, looking at her old sneakers, which fastened with Velcro straps and were pretty ratty compared to her new red Keds.

The phone rang then, so I said, "Come on, Jenny. Race you to the telephone."

Giggling, we ran down to the kitchen.

Guess who was on the phone. Logan.

"Logan, I'm — I'm busy now," I said.

"*Okay.*"

We hung up, and I felt stung, but Jenny was my responsibility, so we went back to her room.

"Your mom sure has been buying you a lot of stuff, Jen," I ventured. I was making every effort not to think about Logan.

"Yup. It's big-girl stuff. Mommy says the baby won't know how to do anything for itself." (Apparently even Jenny didn't know whether she would have a little sister or a little brother.) "So Mommy will be busy, and I'll have to be a big girl."

Since Jenny did not look too happy about this, I said, "You sure are lucky — new shoes, earrings — and all because of the baby."

"Yeah. Mommy wants to make sure I'll like that baby."

Whoa. Had Jenny just said what I thought she said? It sounded as if she *knew* she was being bribed to get along with the new baby.

Mrs. P. certainly had an interesting method for dealing with sibling rivalry.

Jenny showed me two more things that her mother had bought her. Then I helped her to brush her teeth, wash her face, and finally climb into bed. After just a few pages of Babar, Jenny's eyes began to close, so we said good night. I turned out her light, and then I tiptoed out of her room, leaving the door open a crack.

The phone rang immediately. I raced downstairs and picked it up.

It was guess who.

"Jenny asleep yet?" asked Logan.

"Yup. She fell asleep pretty quickly."

"Oh. Well, just checking to see how the job is going."

"It's *fine*."

"*Okay*."

Twenty minutes later, the phone rang again. I knew I should be professional and say, "Hello, Prezziosos' residence." Instead I said, "Hi, Logan."

"You knew it was me?" He sounded surprised.

"I had this feeling."

"Jenny still asleep?"

"Yes."

"So. How about a date? There must be some

evening when you're not baby-sitting."

I hesitated.

"Just tell me when you're free," said Logan.

I told him I'd be free the next night.

"Great. We'll do movies and a pizza. It's all set."

All set by Logan, I couldn't help thinking. What had happened to *me* in our relationship?

CHAPTER 2

I must be the world's biggest wimp. It wasn't that I didn't want to go to a movie with Logan. It was that I felt I had let myself get talked into it. Logan was trying so hard. Why did he need to do that? Had he always been like that? I tried to remember. I didn't think so. Then again, when two people are having problems, it's hard to tell who has changed. Usually, I supposed, they both have. So how had *I* changed? Was I more independent than I used to be? Was I sending Logan mixed signals? Maybe. I wanted to be with him — but I didn't want to lose myself in him.

There was just one thing to do — call a friend and talk about it. As a baby-sitter, I knew the call would have to be short. (It's not a good idea to tie up a client's phone line with personal calls. The parents might be trying to call in to check on things.) So I would have to choose just the right person to talk to — some-

11

one who knows about boys. I consider all the girls in the Baby-sitters Club my friends, and Dawn and Kristy Thomas are my best friends. However, Claudia Kishi and Stacey McGill definitely know the most about boys. I tried Stacey first. Her line was busy. So I called Claudia on her private phone.

I complained to her for about five minutes.

Claud listened patiently, but she didn't have any suggestions. That was okay. I had wanted a solution, but I knew the problem was mine, and I would have to work it out myself. Anyway, I was glad about one thing. I was glad that I had so many friends — so many people I could call on. And that's due mostly to the Baby-sitters Club, which is more of a business than a club. My friends and I baby-sit for children in our neighborhoods. We earn a lot of money doing this and we're good at it. I guess it's because we all love children so much. We're the kind of sitters who really get involved with the children we care for.

Let me tell you about my friends, the BSC members. I'll start with Kristy Thomas, for two reasons. One, she is my oldest friend in the world. (I mean, we're the same age, but we've known each other since we were born.) Two, Kristy had the idea for the BSC, organized it, and got it running. That's just the way Kristy is. She's a doer, an organizer, and she's got a mind full of ideas — which she usually carries out. She's also got a big mouth. I don't mean that she blabs on and on and won't stop talking. I mean that she doesn't always think before she speaks. If something pops into her head, she says it. Occasionally, she hurts people's feelings, although she never intends to.

Kristy is part of the most unusual family I know. She used to be part of a regular family — a mother, a father, two older brothers, and a baby brother named David Michael. Then, shortly after David Michael was born, Mr. Thomas walked out on his family. He just *left* them. Kristy and I lived next door to each other then (and across the street from Claudia), so I know how hard this was for her family. But Mrs. Thomas pulled things together quickly. She got a good job and she managed to hold her family together. Then, when Kristy and I were twelve and in seventh grade, Mrs. Thomas began to be serious about Watson Brewer, this man she'd been going out with. Watson (most of us refer to him as Watson because that's what Kristy calls him) just happens to be a millionaire. He lives in a mansion across town in a much wealthier neighborhood than the one Kristy and I lived in. And at the end of school last year, he and

Mrs. Thomas decided to get married. So they did!

Watson moved the Thomases out of their cramped house and into his huge one. You'd think Kristy would have just *died* to be living in a mansion with bedrooms galore and a rich stepfather, but she wasn't too happy at first. I think that was just because there were too many changes in her life. Not only did she acquire a stepfather and move out of the house in which she'd grown up, but she acquired some other family members, too. First of all, Watson has two kids — Karen, who's seven, and Andrew, who's almost five. Kristy didn't want to like them, but she couldn't help it. They're too adorable. Now she's wild about them. And she even complains that she doesn't see them enough. (Karen and Andrew only live with their father every other weekend and for two weeks during the summer.) *Then*, after Watson and Kristy's mother had been married for awhile, they adopted a two-year-old girl from Vietnam. They named her Emily Michelle. And talk about adorable, well, Emily is right up there with Karen and Andrew. When Emily was adopted, *another* member joined the Thomas/Brewer household. That was Nannie, Kristy's grandmother. She moved in to help with Emily while Watson and Kristy's mom are at work, and to help run the household. Everyone just loves Nannie. She is very special.

Back to Kristy. Kristy has brown hair and brown eyes. She and I look sort of alike. We're both short, although I'm taller than Kristy. And Kristy doesn't need to wear a bra yet, which bothers her. She's a tomboy, and she started a softball team for kids in the neighborhood. The name of her team is Kristy's Krushers. Kristy has a boyfriend, too, although she won't admit it often. He's Bart, the coach of a rival softball team!

It's hard to tell you about Kristy without telling you about me. I guess that's because she's one of my best friends, and because we have a lot in common. In other ways, we're very different, though. (Maybe there's something to the saying that opposites attract.) Anyway, you already know a little about me: that I have brown hair and eyes, and I'm short; that I have a stepmother, and a stepsister named Dawn, who's my other best friend; and that I have a kitten named Tigger, and a boyfriend named Logan with whom I'm having some problems right now.

Here are some other things about me. I'm *extremely* shy and sensitive (that's where Kristy and I are opposites), I'm romantic, and I cry

15

easily. My dad raised me since the time my mother died. That was when I was quite young. Dad was very strict. He made up lots of rules, such as I was not allowed to ride my bike downtown, even when all of my friends were able to. He even picked out my clothes and made me wear my hair in braids. I looked like a real baby at the beginning of seventh grade. Kristy didn't mind that. She isn't — and never has been — interested in clothes. (She just wears jeans and stuff.) But *I* was interested in dressing more stylishly (or at least not like a first-grader), and I wanted my hair *out* of braids. Well, sometime during seventh grade, I was able to prove to my dad that I wasn't a baby, and he started letting up on me. He loosened the rules, allowed me to wear my hair down, and even allowed me to pick out my own clothes. (I am *not* allowed to get my ears pierced, though. But that's okay. I'm not sure I want holes punched through my ears. Besides, Kristy doesn't have pierced ears, either.)

So that's me.

Now, just like it was hard to tell you about Kristy without telling you about me, it's hard to tell you about me without telling you about Dawn, since she's my stepsister. For starters, Dawn is *gorgeous*. She has long, pale blonde

16

hair and sparkly blue eyes. Dawn is our California girl. She grew up outside of L.A., and lived there until her parents got divorced. After the divorce, Mrs. Schafer (Dawn's mother) moved Dawn and Dawn's younger brother, Jeff, all the way to Stoneybrook. That's because Mrs. Schafer grew up here and her parents still live here. Of course, the move was difficult for Dawn and Jeff. They switched from a warm climate to a cold one (cold in the winter, anyway), and they had to leave all their friends behind. Dawn adjusted to this pretty well, but Jeff never did, and after awhile, he moved back to California to live with Mr. Schafer. This is not an ideal situation, but it's the way things are. Dawn and Jeff frequently fly across country to visit the other half of their family.

I think one of the reasons Dawn adjusted to the move so well is because she's an individualist. She's independent and usually doesn't care what people think about her. She eats what she wants (health food) and dresses the way she likes. (My friends and I think of Dawn's style as California casual.) Dawn loves mysteries and reading ghost stories, so you can imagine that she was delighted to find that the old farmhouse her mother bought came complete with a secret passage. The passage leads from Dawn's bedroom (the entrance is concealed in the paneling) to the barn on our property, and it was part of the Underground Railroad long, long ago. Guess what. The passage may even be *haunted!*

Here's how Dawn and I got to be stepsisters. First we became friends (right after Dawn moved to Connecticut), then we realized that my father and Dawn's mother had gone to Stoneybrook High together, and then, by looking through their old yearbooks, we discovered that they had been in love. We found out that they wanted to get married, but Dawn's grandparents didn't think my dad was good enough for their daughter, so they sent Sharon off to college in California. That's where Sharon met Mr. Schafer, and where they married and had Dawn and Jeff. Anyway, when Dawn and I realized that our parents had been in love, we were quick to get them back together. They had an on-again, off-again romance for awhile, but finally they got married. The rest is Schafer/Spier history.

Claudia Kishi, another BSC member, is the one I spoke to on the phone when I felt as if I was wimping out with Logan. Although Claudia grew up with Kristy and me, she's always been more mature than we have. She wears the trendiest clothes you can imagine, and she is *so cool*. A typical Claudia outfit might be black leggings, a baggy black-and-white shirtdress, low black shoes, and big wild earrings for her pierced ears. This outfit would be particularly striking on Claud because of her looks. She's as gorgeous as Dawn, but in a different way. Claudia is Japanese-American. She's got silky, jet-black hair; dark, dark, almond-shaped eyes; and this creamy complexion. The fact that her complexion is flawless comes as a great surprise to everyone, since Claud is the biggest junk-food nut we've ever known. If it tastes good and is bad for you, Claud likes it. Of course, her parents don't approve of the habit, so Claudia has to hide her junk food. She's got it stashed all over her bedroom — in drawers, under pillows, behind books on her shelves. It's amazing.

Poor Claud. She has another habit her parents don't approve of — she reads Nancy Drew books. So she has to hide her books, too. The reason her parents don't approve of Nancy Drew is that they feel Claud should be reading something more challenging. *I* think she should be allowed to read what she wants to read. If she didn't read her mysteries, she wouldn't read anything at all. Claud is not a great student. She's *smart*, but she does poorly in school, especially in math, reading, and spelling. Her teachers say she doesn't apply herself, but if I were Claud, I'd be just plain nervous about school. That's because Claud has to follow in the footsteps of her older sister, Janine, who is a true genius. Janine is in high school, but she takes courses at the local community college. Plus, she is always winning awards for her schoolwork. Luckily, Claudia has one true talent. She is an artist. She can do just about anything — paint, sketch, sculpt, even make jewelry. She makes a lot of her own jewelry, and sometimes makes jewelry for other people.

Claudia's best friend is Stacey McGill. Like Dawn, Stacey is a newcomer to Stoneybrook. She and her parents moved here from New York City just before Stacey was to begin seventh grade. Stacey had grown up in New York (she is *so* lucky) and she's as sophisticated as Claudia, which may be why they get along so well. Stacey also wears super-trendy clothes — layers on layers, hats, pins, cowboy boots, that sort of thing. Plus she's allowed to have her blonde hair permed and she likes to wear nail polish, usually with sparkles in it.

Stacey may seem glamorous, but her life has definitely *not* been that way. Stacey's had a tough time, with both her family and her health. See, Stacey had moved to Stoneybrook because the company her father works for had transferred his job to Stamford, which is a city not far away. The McGills had been here for less than a year when the company transferred Mr. McGill *back* to New York. We were all sad to see Stacey leave (Claudia was especially sad), but then something traumatic happened. Stacey's parents decided to get a divorce. Even worse, Mr. McGill wanted to stay in New York with his job, while Mrs. McGill wanted to return to Stoneybrook. So Stacey had to decide whether to live in the city in which she'd grown up or to move back to Stoneybrook with her mom. Luckily for Claud and all us BSC members, Stacey chose Connecticut, but she still visits her father pretty frequently. Going back and forth between Connecticut and New York is not always easy, though.

As for Stacey's health, she has a disease called diabetes, and she has a severe form of it. (She said something recently about being a "brittle" diabetic, but I don't know what that is.) Anyway, when someone has diabetes, it means that a gland in the body, the pancreas, stops making something called insulin. Insulin breaks down sugar in the blood. Without insulin, a person's blood sugar level gets all out of whack and he (or she) could even go into a diabetic coma, which is very dangerous. So poor Stacey has to *inject* herself with insulin (ew, *ew*, EW!) every day, and stay on a strict diet. On her diet she can eat practically no sweets, and she has to count calories to make sure she consumes the proper number — without fail. Stacey has been looking thin lately and feeling tired. Sometimes we worry about her.

The last two members of the BSC are younger than Dawn, Kristy, Stacey, Claudia, and I. Their names are Mallory Pike and Jessi Ramsey, and they're both eleven and in sixth grade. They are also best friends, and like most best friends they have some things in common, yet are very different in many ways. Here are the ways in which they're different:

Mallory comes from a *huge* family. She has seven brothers and sisters! And three of them are identical triplets (boys). Jessi comes from a more regular-sized family. She has a younger sister and a baby brother. (Mal and Jessi each live with both of their parents, plus Jessi's Aunt Cecelia lives at the Ramseys' house.)

Jessi is thinking of becoming a professional ballet dancer one day, while Mal is pretty sure she's going to write and illustrate children's books after she goes to college. Boy, you should see Jessi dance. She is *really* talented. She dances *en pointe* (that means *on toe*), she takes lessons at a special ballet school in Stamford, *and* she has danced lead parts in lots of productions before big audiences. Mallory is talented, too, but she's more private about her stories and drawings. We don't get to see many of them, but when we do, we're impressed.

One last difference between Jessi and Mal — Jessi is black (with long, long dancer's legs, and beautiful eyes), and Mal is white (and not feeling too pretty these days. She wears glasses and braces, and has unruly red hair).

Here are the ways in which Mal and Jessi are similar:

They both like to read, especially horse stories by Marguerite Henry. And they're each the oldest kid in their family but feel that their parents treat them like babies. For instance, the Pikes absolutely will not allow Mallory to wear contacts instead of glasses. However, in a recent parent-daughter breakthrough, Mal and Jessi convinced their parents to allow them to have their ears pierced. So that was something. Maybe contacts for Mallory will come next.

I feel awfully grateful to have so many good

friends. If there were such a thing, I think the BSC members would be the Seven Musketeers. Oh, sure, we've had our arguments and fights, but we're usually there for each other, through thick and thin. And we're pretty understanding of each other.

CHAPTER 3

"*What is that?*" I asked, looking horrified.

Claudia looked pretty horrified herself.

The two of us were in her room, along with Dawn and Mallory, waiting for a meeting of the BSC to begin, and I had just pointed to something. It was a large, sticky-looking brown stain on Claudia's bedspread, and it was only partially covered by the quilt folded at the end of the bed.

"Oh, lord," said Claudia, examining it. Then she leaned over and smelled it.

"Gross!" exclaimed Mal. "How can you do that?"

But Claudia looked relieved. "It's only chocolate," she said. "I hid a candy bar under the quilt. I guess it got a little warm in there."

"What are your parents going to say when they see it?" asked Dawn.

Claudia shrugged. She pulled the quilt over

25

the stain to hide it. "I'll worry about that some other time."

Claudia flopped onto her bed and leaned against the wall. She was looking especially acute that day. (*Acute* means *cool*. My friends and I make up words all the time, and only we know what they mean. *Distant* and *dibble* also mean *cool*.) Claud was wearing an oversized raspberry-colored shirt, a short black skirt, and black leggings (the layered look). On her feet were black cowboy boots, and dangling from an earcuff was a huge collection of beads and stones. (Claud does have pierced ears, but the holes were empty.)

I settled myself in my usual spot on Claud's bed (beside Claud), but only after she had covered up the chocolate stain. Compared to Claudia, I looked like a complete nerd, even though I was wearing one of my better outfits: blue print pants that were wide on top but narrowed to cuffs at the ankles, and a short-cropped T-shirt with the sleeves rolled up and this acute picture of a cactus wearing a cowboy boot.

Kristy came thundering up the stairs and into Claud's room then. (There's no mistaking when Kristy is on her way to club headquarters.) "Where is everybody?" she asked immediately. "It's already five twenty-five."

"They'll get here," replied Claud calmly.

And Claud was right. By 5:29, we were all in our places. Dawn and Claudia and I were sitting in a row on Claud's bed; Jessi and Mal were cross-legged on the floor, leaning against the bed; Stacey was straddling Claud's desk chair backward; and Kristy — our president — was sitting in a director's chair, wearing a visor, a pencil stuck over one ear.

She looked almost regal, even though she was just wearing blue jeans, a turtleneck shirt, and her running shoes.

As soon as the numbers on Claud's digital alarm clock changed from 5:29 to 5:30, Kristy said loudly, "Okay. Come to order!"

Kristy, being the president, gets to lead the meetings. Anyway, the original idea for the Baby-sitters Club was hers. See, a year or so ago, when Kristy still lived across the street from Claud, and before Mrs. Thomas had married Watson Brewer, Kristy and her older brothers took turns baby-sitting for David Michael after school. They didn't mind that arrangement, but of course a day came when all three of them knew they were going to be busy after school, so they wouldn't be able to take care of their little brother. That night, Kristy sat around eating pizza for dinner and watching as her mother made call after call, trying to find someone who could take care of David Michael the next afternoon. And that was how Kristy got her big idea to form a baby-sitting club. If a parent could make one call and reach several sitters at once, it would save time for the parent and also pretty much guarantee him or her a sitter. Someone was bound to be free.

Kristy told her idea to Claudia and me, and we thought it was great. We also thought a fourth member might be a good idea. Three people didn't seem like quite enough. So Claud mentioned that she was getting to be friends with Stacey McGill, a new girl at school. When we found out that Stacey had done a lot of baby-sitting in New York, we invited her to join the club.

Now we had a sitting business — but no one knew about it. We decided to advertise. We told everyone we could think of about the club. We passed out fliers. We even put an ad in the paper. Our ad and the fliers told parents that they could reach us Monday, Wednesday, and Friday afternoons from five-thirty until six at Claudia's house.

Well, at our first meeting, everything went well. We got job calls right away. And the business just kept growing. By the middle of seventh grade we had too *much* business and realized we needed a fifth member. Dawn had just moved here from California then, and she and I were already friends. So Dawn joined the club. Then Stacey had to leave, so we replaced her with both Jessi and Mal. And *then* Stacey returned. Of course, we let her back in the club. Now the club has seven main members (there are two other members who don't come to meetings, but I'll tell you about them later), and we think seven is plenty. Claudia's room is getting crowded!

Everyone in the BSC has a title. For instance, as I mentioned before, Kristy is the president. This is not only because she thought up the business in the first place, but because she gets good ideas and really knows how to run a club (even if she does get bossy sometimes). Kristy makes us keep a club notebook. In the notebook, each of us writes up every single job she goes on. Then, once a week, we're responsible for reading the notebook to see what happened while our friends were sitting. None of us really likes writing up jobs (except maybe Mallory), but we have to admit that finding out how the other sitters solved problems, and what's going on with the kids we sit for, is pretty helpful.

Kristy also decided that we should have a record book in which we keep lists of our clients, their names, addresses, phone numbers, the rates they pay, etc. Plus, we record any money we earn, and on the appointment pages we keep track of when our sitting jobs are.

Another one of Kristy's great ideas was for each of us to make a Kid-Kit. A Kid-Kit is an ordinary cardboard carton that you decorate to look cheerful and pretty and fill with things kids will like, such as our old games, toys, and books, as well as new things that have to be replaced from time to time, like art materials, coloring books, and sticker books. Then we can bring the Kid-Kits on sitting jobs if we want to. (They're especially handy on rainy days.) Kids love them, so their parents are happy, which means our clients will call the BSC again, which means more sitting jobs for us!

The vice-president of the club is Claudia. Since she has her own phone and personal phone number, we use Claudia's bedroom for our headquarters. And since we therefore descend on her three times a week, tie up her phone, and eat her junk food, we felt it was only fair that Claud be our vice-president.

I am the club secretary, and I'm responsible for keeping the record book up-to-date and in order. I'm also responsible for scheduling every single sitting job. There are a lot of details involved here, but I'm good at details. Besides, Kristy thinks I have the neatest handwriting of any of us.

Our treasurer is Stacey. She's a real math brain. *Her* job is to collect our weekly dues, put the money in the treasury (a manila envelope), and hand out money when it's needed — for instance, to buy refills for the Kid-Kits, to help pay Claud's phone bills, and to pay Charlie for driving Kristy to and from meetings now that she lives across town. Stacey also records the money we earn. (This is just for our interest. We don't pool our earnings and then divide it up. The money each of us makes is ours to keep.)

Dawn is the alternate officer of the BSC. That means that she can take over the job of anyone who misses a meeting. She knows the responsibilities of everyone in the club. That way we'll never have to go without a secretary, a treasurer, or etc. Dawn is like an understudy in a play, or a substitute teacher.

Mal and Jessi are our junior officers. This simply means that they're younger than the rest of us, and aren't allowed to sit at night unless they're watching their own brothers and sisters. They can baby-sit after school or on weekend days, though, which is good because it frees us older club members for evening jobs.

Can you believe it? Even with *seven* members of the BSC, people sometimes call and offer us a job that none of us can take. That's because we're so busy. Aside from baby-sitting and homework, most of us have other activities or responsibilities. Jessi takes ballet lessons, Claud goes to art classes, Mallory has appointments with the orthodontist. . . . When we realized that there were going to be occasional times when we'd have to disappoint a client and tell him or her that nobody in the BSC was free to sit, we signed on two associate members. The associate members don't come to meetings, but they are good backups (also good baby-sitters). They're people we can call on in a pinch. One is Shannon Kilbourne, a friend of Kristy's (she lives in Kristy's neighborhood) and the other is . . . Logan Bruno!

Our club is very efficient (thanks mostly to Kristy), and it's businesslike and professional, which is why it's successful.

I am proud to be a member of the BSC.

When Kristy said, "Come to order!" the rest of us sat up a bit straighter. We paid attention to our president.

"Okay," Kristy went on. "It's Monday, dues day. Fork over."

Most of us groaned as we reached into our pockets for money. Stacey, however, passed around the treasury with a gleam in her eye. She *loves* collecting money. (But she hates parting with it. She makes a big production out of withdrawing funds from the treasury each time any of us needs to replace an item in the Kid-Kit or something.)

When the dues had been collected, Kristy said, "Any club business?"

We shook our heads. Things were running smoothly.

"How's Mrs. Prezzioso?" Kristy wanted to know.

"She's fine," I replied. "She's going to have — "

"Don't tell us what the baby's going to be!" shrieked Jessi.

"I wasn't going to. I was just going to say that she's going to have the baby soon. In a few weeks, I think. But she's the same old Mrs. P."

The phone rang then, and Dawn answered it. "Hello, Baby-sitters Club. . . . Oh, hi, Mr. Ohdner. . . . Friday night? . . . Okay. I'll check and call you right back." Dawn hung up the phone and turned to me. "Mr. Ohdner needs a sitter next Friday night from seven until about ten-thirty. Who's free?"

I checked the appointment pages in the record book. "Let's see. You're free, Kristy, and so are you, Stace," I said.

"You take the job," Kristy said to Stacey. "You live much nearer to the Ohdners than I do. Besides, Andrew and Karen will be with us that night. I want to spend some time with them."

That's how we usually handle job calls — no squabbling over who gets one if several of us are free. We know there will be other jobs.

Dawn called Mr. Ohdner back to tell him that Stacey would be sitting on Friday.

As soon as she hung up the phone, it rang again. Then two more times. The meeting was pretty busy. One of the last calls to come in was from Mr. Prezzioso, Jenny's father. He hardly ever calls, so Jessi was surprised when she picked up the phone. "It's *Mister* Prezzioso," she mouthed to the rest of us. Then she went back to the phone call. She was saying, "Three of us? . . . Well, we don't usually take on jobs like that, but this sounds fun. Let me check with the others and call you right back. . . . You're at *work?* Oh, that makes sense." Jessi jotted down a phone number, said good-bye to Mr. P., and hung up.

34

"What was that all about?" asked Kristy.

"Mr. Prezzioso," Jessi said, "is planning a surprise baby shower for Mrs. P. He wants three of us to give him a hand that day — one to watch Jenny, and two to decorate the house while Mrs. P. is being taken out to lunch or something, and also to serve food, clean up, and stuff like that."

"Well, I think we should take the job," said Kristy. "The Prezziosos are good clients, and besides, there is *some* baby-sitting involved." She turned to me. "Are three of us free that day?"

Jessi gave me the date and time of the shower. I checked the appointment pages. Claudia, Stacey, and I were free, so we took the job.

When the meeting was over, Kristy announced, "Good one, you guys!" and sent us all home.

CHAPTER 4

Ahhh.

I had been looking forward to this for a *long* time. It was a snowy Saturday afternoon, and I had already finished my weekend homework. I didn't have a baby-sitting job or *any-thing* to do. I mean, anything I *had* to do. In other words, I was free, free, free. And with the snow falling outside, I felt that this was the perfect afternoon to do cozy indoor things. Let's see. I could work on the sweater I was knitting. Or I could start a present for the Prezzioso baby — maybe a knitted blanket, or a hat and booties.

Or I could read.

That was what I really wanted to do. Dad had built a fire in the living-room fireplace, and I was just dying to lie in front of it and reread *Wuthering Heights*. I'd read it about three times, but *Wuthering Heights* is like *To Kill a Mockingbird*. You simply can't read it often enough. In fact, I think both books get better every time you read them.

So I found my copy of *Wuthering Heights*, grabbed the comforter off my bed, and ran downstairs. Then I sat in front of the fire, the comforter around my shoulders, and began the book once more. "1801. I have just returned from a visit to my landlord. . . ." As soon as I read those words I was transplanted from our living room to old England, the moors, Heathcliff, Cathy, and romance.

The house was quiet except for the crackling fire. Dawn had gone over to Claudia's to learn how to make jewelry (she likes beaded jewelry), Dad was in the den doing some work (he's a lawyer), and Sharon was running errands.

I was gigundo happy, as Karen Brewer would say.

I had been enjoying the book, the fire, and the quiet for about ten minutes when the doorbell rang. I sighed, then called, "Dad, I'll get it!" and walked reluctantly to the front door.

I peeked through one of the side windows. Guess who was standing on our steps.

Logan.

He hadn't said anything about coming over that day. At least, I didn't think he had.

I opened the door.

"Surprise!" said Logan, grinning, except that with his gentle accent it sounded more like he'd said, "Supprazz!"

I just stood there. Half of my mind was back in 1801 with Heathcliff and Cathy and the moors. The other half was trying to figure out what Logan was doing here.

After a few seconds, Logan said, "Aren't you going to let me in?"

"Oh! Oh, sure." I stepped aside.

Logan entered our front hall, but he didn't bother to take off his coat. "Let's go out," he said. "It's a perfect snow day in the park. Bring your ice skates." (Logan's skates were slung over his shoulder.) When I didn't say anything right away, Logan went on. "I know you're free. Dawn told me you were looking forward to this afternoon."

"I — I was."

"So come on," said Logan. "Ice-skating, a walk in the snow . . ."

I looked over my shoulder at the fire and my open book. Then I looked back at Logan. He seemed so excited and happy. He added that he had planned a romantic afternoon, just for us.

How could I turn him down?

I couldn't. "Dad?" I called. "Logan's here.

We're going to go to the park for a few hours, okay?"

"Okay," replied my father.

So I found my skates, bundled up, and set off with Logan. I had to admit that walking through the light snow that was falling *was* nice. Romantic, too.

The walk to the park took about ten minutes, and Logan talked most of the way there. That was okay with me. I didn't feel much like talking.

When we reached the park, my body still half at home by the fire, Logan said, "Boy, it's crowded today."

Stoneybrook's little park *was* crowded. It was colorful, too. Kids wearing bright ski jackets were playing everywhere. They looked like confetti against the sharp, white snow.

"Now, I've got everything planned," Logan informed me. "Ice-skating first."

"Okay," I replied, beginning to feel even better about the afternoon.

Logan and I sat next to each other on a bench by the frozen pond. Laughing, I laced up Logan's skates for him, while he laced up mine. Then we tottered arm-in-arm to the edge of the pond and stepped gingerly onto the ice. In a flash, Logan was flying me around the pond, holding tightly to my hand. Or maybe *I* was gripping *his*. I am not a good skater. In fact, unlike Kristy the tomboy, I'm no good at sports at all.

I think something is wrong with my coordination.

"Logan!" I said, gasping. "Slow down!"

"Oh, you want a leisurely turn around the ice? That's a good idea. Then everyone can see what a great couple we make."

Logan dropped my hand, and we linked arms again. We skated around and around. Sometimes we had to dodge little kids, and twice I almost fell, but still skating was pleasant. . . . Until my toes began to freeze.

I skated slower and slower. I could barely feel my feet.

"Mary Anne?" said Logan questioningly.

"Can we stop now?" I asked. "My toes are — "

"Sure. I'm tired of skating, too," said Logan. Whew! What a relief.

Logan and I glided back to the bench, untied our laces, and pulled our skates off. "Ahh," I said, rubbing each foot between my hands. A little feeling began to come back. I wriggled my toes. That was more like it.

As soon as I'd put my boots on, Logan jumped up, skates slung over his shoulder again. "Next we're going to be kids!" he exclaimed. "Look over there."

I turned in the direction that Logan was pointing and saw a group of children building a snowman.

We didn't know a single one of them, but Logan trotted over to them anyway, and I followed him.

"Need a little help with that?" Logan asked two girls who were valiantly trying to lift the snowman's head onto his body.

The girls looked up at Logan. "Sure!" they said.

Logan plopped the head onto the body.

"Thanks! Will you help us find some sticks and pebbles and things so we can finish our snowman? We want him to look just right."

"Of course," Logan replied. "Come on, Mary Anne."

Logan wandered happily around the park, looking for twigs. I limped after him. Once again my feet were starting to freeze. "Logan, I'm — "

But Logan didn't hear me. He was too busy putting a face on the snowman. When the snowman was finally finished, Logan grabbed my hand and pulled me to a quiet area of the park. I could hardly move. You need your toes for balance, and I couldn't feel mine.

"Let's make snow angels," Logan said, and flopped faceup onto the snow.

"Logan — "

"Come on. We're kids again today, remember?"

"But Logan, I'm cold."

"Oh. Well, let's go over to the snack bar and get some hot chocolate. My treat."

I hobbled to the snack bar and allowed Logan to buy two hot chocolates with whipped cream on top. He carried them to a bench and handed me one of the steaming cups. I had taken my mittens off, and for a moment, I just held the cup, trying to warm my hands.

By now, my feet weren't the only frozen parts of my body. The rest of me was pretty cold, too. In fact, my teeth were chattering, which made drinking sort of interesting.

We finished our hot chocolates and then walked slowly through the park. Logan kept admiring the white-frosted tree branches, the mounds of snow that were actually buried bushes, and icicles that hung from unlikely places. Once, we saw a male cardinal fly from one tree to another, a splash of red against the gray sky.

Even I was enchanted by that and let out an "Ooh."

Logan looked at me happily.

I think he was going to tell me something, but I just had to say, "Logan, I'm really sorry, but I'm *freez*ing."

"You can't be *too* cold, Mary Anne. I don't feel cold." (Logan wasn't even wearing his gloves.)

Why couldn't I feel cold? I *was* cold. I get cold easily.

Logan was heading for the pond again. "One more time on the ice?" he said.

The *ice?* No, no, no . . .

It was time to speak up — and be forceful. This was not going to be easy. I have trouble being forceful with anyone. But since my body was turning into an iceberg, I said, "Logan, can we go home *now?* I really am freezing."

Logan took a hard look at me. At last he said, "O*kay*," in a sort of huffy voice, and marched toward the park entrance, leaving me to follow him.

All I could do was sigh.

CHAPTER 5

                                    Saturday

I may be thirteen, but I still get excited about Valentine's Day, just like I did when I was little. So I was pretty happy today when I was left in charge of my younger brothers and sisters and discovered that David Michael wanted to make valentines for the kids in his class. That was a fun project.

But I had a problem on my hands, too: Karen. She and Andrew are here for the weekend, and Karen has a "boyfriend" she's fighting with. She said they were going to get married, but now the wedding is off. Karen was mopey, so I tried to talk to her, control Andrew, who was being pesty (not like himself at all), and oversee David Michael — and Emily, who likes anything involving glue and glitter. Especially glue.

Right after lunch on Saturday, Kristy's grandmother was picked up by some friends who were taking her to the movies, Watson and Kristy's mom left to go shopping in a nearby town, Charlie went off somewhere in the Junk Bucket (his car), and Sam headed for school to attend a special meeting.

So Kristy baby-sat for David Michael, Emily, Andrew, and Karen. David Michael and Andrew were wound up. The day was gray and sloppy, so they'd been cooped up all morning and had no chance of going out in the afternoon, either. They ran screaming through the house. They could make a circle by starting in the front hall, tearing through the dining room, into the kitchen, through another hallway, through the living room, and back to the front hall. They looked as if they were chasing each other, but Kristy couldn't tell who was chasing whom. Sometimes Andrew was just in front of David Michael, and sometimes it was the other way around. Neither of them was tagging or tackling the other. Kristy guessed they were just having a let-your-energy-out-however-you-can chase.

The chase had been going on for about five minutes when Emily joined in. She's a bit unsteady on her legs, so she couldn't keep up with the boys very well, but she can scream along with the best of them. And she figured out the circle through the house that her brothers were making. So she chugged along, giggling, while David Michael and Andrew kept passing her. The "chase" reminded Kristy of that story about the tortoise and the hare.

Ordinarily, Kristy would have put a stop to the running around. (It was the kind of indoor activity that could lead to tears, or to a knocked-over-and-broken something.) But the kids were having so much fun that Kristy let them go for awhile. Besides, she was worried about Karen.

Karen had been sitting on the bottom step of the stairs since before everyone had left. Her chin was resting in her hands, and she seemed oblivious to the three children who kept roaring by her. She just sat, looking thoughtful. No, Kristy decided. Not thoughtful, sad. Karen looked truly sad.

"Karen?" said Kristy.

Karen didn't answer. She didn't move, except for her eyes. She looked up at Kristy. And her eyes seemed to say, "Everything in my life is wrong."

"Come on, Karen," said Kristy, reaching for one of Karen's hands. "Let's have a talk. We'll go into the den, so we can escape your brothers and sister."

Karen stood up wordlessly and let Kristy lead her into the den. Kristy pushed the door closed — but not all the way. She needed to keep her ears open for the other kids.

"So what's going on?" Kristy asked Karen. "I've hardly ever seen you look like this."

"Like what?" asked Karen. She was curled into a tight ball at one end of the couch. Kristy was sitting at the other end, but Karen wouldn't look at her.

"As sad as a rain cloud," Kristy replied, trying to get a smile out of Karen.

No such luck. All Karen replied was, "I *feel* as sad as a rain cloud."

"Why?" asked Kristy. "What's wrong?"

Karen shrugged. Then tears filled her eyes. "It's Ricky," she finally managed to say.

"Ricky Torres?" asked Kristy, who tries to keep up with Karen and Andrew's lives, even though she doesn't see them too often.

Karen nodded miserably. Her eyes were red, but no tears had fallen.

"Is he teasing you again?" Kristy demanded.

Karen shook her head. "It's much worse than that."

"What, then?"

"Ricky and I were supposed to get married. He asked me, and everything. I even have a ring for him. But we had a fight and now we're not talking to each other."

"What was the fight about?" Kristy wanted to know.

Karen squirmed. "It was kind of silly, I guess."

"Most fights start out that way," Kristy told her sister.

At that moment, she and Karen heard a thud. In less than a second (well, maybe I'm exaggerating) Kristy had flung open the door to the den and was racing along the kids' chase route. She was relieved not to hear tears.

"What happened?" she called.

"Emily lost control," David Michael called back. "She slipped on a rug and fell, but she's okay."

Kristy had reached the living room by then and saw Andrew helping Emily to her feet. Emily was smiling. "More!" she cried.

Kristy smiled, too, but had to say, "Sorry. *No* more. No more of this game, Emily. Or for you two, either," she added, looking at Andrew and David Michael.

"Aww," said Andrew.

"Bullfrogs," said David Michael. Then he added, "What are we going to do now?"

"Well," Kristy began thoughtfully, "a certain holiday is coming up."

A pause. Then, "Valentine's Day!" shrieked David Michael.

"How about making cards for the kids in your class?" suggested Kristy.

"Okay," said David Michael.

But Andrew said, "I already made cards. Karen and I made them with Mommy. We made a lot."

"Maybe you could help Emily, then," said Kristy. "She's never made a valentine before. I'm sure she'd have fun if you worked with her."

So it was settled. Kristy spread newspapers over the kitchen table and got out the stash of art supplies that are kept in the den. (By the way, Kristy walked into the den, loaded up the supplies, left — and Karen never budged. She was still a little ball in the corner of the couch.)

Kristy left Karen there. They would finish their talk later. She put the supplies on the kitchen table and let David Michael, Andrew, and Emily go to work.

David Michael immediately reached for red construction paper and the pair of safety scissors. He cut out a heart, took a black felt-tipped marker, and wrote on the heart:

HAPPY VALENTINE'S DAY TO YOU!
HAPPY VALENTINE'S DAY TO YOU!
YOU LOOK LIKE A MONKEY,
AND YOU SMELL LIKE ONE, TOO.

"David Michael!" exclaimed Kristy. "Who are you giving *that* to?"

"Blair D'Angelo. He's a bully. He teases all the girls." David Michael paused. Then he went on. "Hmm. Maybe I better not sign this one."

Kristy just shook her head. Then she went to the den to try to pry Karen out. "Come into the kitchen with the rest of us," she said. "I know you've already made valentines, but I need to keep an eye on the others, especially Emily, and I want to talk to you, too."

Karen heaved a great sigh and then got up. She followed Kristy into the kitchen. Since the boys and Emily were working on one side of the table, Kristy pulled the empty bench a little away, for privacy, and then straddled one end. Karen sat facing her. Now Kristy could keep an eye on the card-makers and talk to Karen at the same time.

"Okay," Kristy began. "What was your stupid fight about?"

"My fight with Ricky? Well . . ." Karen looked down at her hands. "Everyone in our class got invited to Pamela Harding's birthday party. And you know she doesn't like Hannie or Nancy or me or Ricky — or most of the kids. But her parents made her invite the whole class, and *our* parents made us go to the party. *But*," Karen continued, "Ricky and I decided to do mean things to Pamela to ruin the party. Ricky even said he would give Pamela a snake as her present.

"But he didn't. He didn't do one mean thing. He gave her a really nice present. And he even smiled at Pamela."

"Maybe you're a little jealous," said Kristy gently.

"Maybe. I don't know. Anyway, we stopped talking to each other, and then Ricky poured ink on a drawing I was making. He did it *on purpose*. So I put chewed-up gum in his desk, and . . . everything's awful. I guess we won't be getting married now. But I don't know for sure, since we aren't speaking."

"That's hard," said Kristy. "You must feel pretty bad. But you know what? These things have a way of resolving themselves."

"What?" said Karen.

"I mean, they have a way of working themselves out."

"Oh." Karen stared off into space.

"Andrew, cut it out!" David Michael cried suddenly.

Kristy looked up in time to see Andrew dropping glitter into David Michael's hair. David Michael was frantically brushing it out.

"You look cool!" Andrew was saying. "You're a punk rocker!"

"Andrew," said Kristy. "I don't think David Michael likes what you're doing. Besides — look at Emily. She could use some help." Emily was having a little trouble with the glue. Somehow she had unscrewed the cap. Glue was everywhere, but mostly on her hands — and any place she touched. At the moment, she was brushing her hair out of her eyes, so her face and hair were gluey.

"Uh-oh," muttered Kristy. This was a job for her, not for Andrew. "Bath time, Emily," said Kristy.

"NO!" cried Emily.

"I am so sad," said Karen.

"You're a monkey-face, David Michael!" exclaimed Andrew.

"Shut up," David Michael replied.

"In this house, we do not say 'shut up,' " Kristy reminded her brother.

"But Andrew called me a monkey-face."

"Okay, okay." Kristy led Emily to the sink. "I'll wash you off here for now," she told her. "Andrew, please stop pestering your brother. David Michael, calm down. You've made five valentines already, and four of them are gorgeous, so keep going. Karen, why don't you find a book and I'll read to you guys in the kitchen while David Michael and Emily work on their cards."

Karen heaved a great sigh as if Kristy had just asked her to clean the entire house. Then she stood up slowly, left the kitchen, and after ten minutes returned with a copy of *The Dead Bird*.

"Couldn't you have found something more cheerful?" asked Kristy.

"No," Karen answered, and sighed again.

Kristy almost smiled. The trials and tribulations of being seven, she thought. She began to read the story, and the rest of the afternoon passed uneventfully.

CHAPTER 6

"Hello? I'm home!" I called.

It was a Friday night and I had just returned from a date with Logan. We had planned to eat dinner at a coffee shop downtown and then go to the movies. I had told Dad and Sharon that I would be home around eleven.

It was ten minutes of nine.

The date had not gone well.

When we reached the coffee shop, we were shown to a booth. (*That* was okay.) Then we had opened our menus and looked and looked. The menus were huge, but I chose my meal fairly quickly. I already knew what I wanted. I'd been wanting it all afternoon — a grilled cheese-and-tomato sandwich and a vanilla milkshake.

Soon Logan closed his menu, and right away a waiter materialized. "What can I do for you?" he asked with a smile.

I opened my mouth to give my order, but

54

before I could make a sound, Logan said, "I'll have the cheeseburger deluxe and a large Coke, and my friend will have the same."

I just looked at Logan. It's true that I often order a cheeseburger and a Coke, but that wasn't what I wanted. Too late. The waiter had scribbled down the order and left.

"Logan," I said, "that, um, wasn't what I wanted."

"No? Sorry. Maybe we can get the waiter back."

"That's okay," I mumbled, which got dinner off to an awkward start. We didn't talk much during it.

But afterward, Logan perked up a little. He checked his watch, rubbed his hands together, and announced, "All *right!* Time to go see *Halloween, Part Three*."

"*Halloween?*"

"Yeah. I know it's been out awhile, but I haven't seen it, and it's playing right around the corner. I hope *you* haven't seen it, Mary Anne."

"No, I haven't. . . . I thought we were going to see *The Music Man*. It's playing at the oldies theater."

"*The Music Man* is a kids' movie," Logan informed me.

"But the *Halloween* movies are so gross."

55

"So what do you want to do?"

"I — I guess I want to go home," I replied.

Logan glared at me. Then he stood up and huffed off to the pay phone to call his parents and ask one of them to pick us up.

So we didn't see a movie, and that was why I arrived home at ten to nine instead of at eleven. That was also why I wasn't in a particularly good mood, and possibly why I was tired.

Logan was wearing me out.

Dad was the only one who answered when I announced that I had returned. "Mary Anne? Is that you? You're home early. Come and talk to me. I'm in the den."

I entered the den and flopped into an easy chair. "Where are Sharon and Dawn?" I asked. "Did they go out?"

"They just ran to the grocery. They'll be back soon. Actually I'm glad you and I have a few moments alone together. I want to talk to you."

Ordinarily those awful words ("I want to talk to you") would have set me on edge right away. They never mean anything good. But my mind was still on my "date" with Logan. Nothing could be worse than this evening, I thought.

So I said simply, "Okay."

Dad cleared his throat. (He's not good at having talks.) "Well," he began, "I think you and Logan are getting — I mean, that you and Logan are spending too much time together."

I nodded.

"I'm not *worried* about you. I'm just concerned because you're not around very often, and . . . I miss you." (I knew those words were difficult for Dad to say.) "Also, you don't seem terribly happy lately. And you got a C on your last English test. That's not like you."

"I know," I said.

"'So I think that you and Logan should cut back on the amount of time you spend together. I know this is hard for you to hear, but this is the way it's going to be. If necessary, we can decide on exactly how many hours you and Logan may spend together every week."

"No," I said. "We don't need to do that. I *have* been seeing too much of Logan. I'm tired. And I can't believe I got a C on that test. You're right, Dad."

My father looked so taken aback that I laughed.

"I'm *right?!* When are parents ever right?" Dad teased me.

"Hardly ever," I replied. "This is just one of those rare times."

It was Dad's turn to laugh.

"I'll call Logan tonight and talk to him," I told Dad. "I — "

But we heard the back door open then. Sharon and Dawn had come home. Our talk was over. I think Dad and I both felt relieved.

"Hey," said Dawn when she saw me. "You're home early. What happened?"

"Let's go upstairs and talk," I replied. (I caught Dad and Sharon raising their eyebrows at each other.)

Dawn followed me into my bedroom and sat in the armchair while I lay on my stomach on the bed.

"So what happened?" Dawn asked again.

"The date was a flop," I said simply.

Dawn frowned.

I told her about ordering dinner and about the movie and everything. Then I went on. "When I came home, Dad wanted to have a talk with me."

"Oh," said Dawn. "Did Mom and I interrupt something?"

"Not really," I replied. "We were about finished."

"What did your dad want to talk to you about?"

"Logan and me. He thinks we're spending too much time together."

"Uh-oh. What's he going to do?"

"Nothing. I agreed with him."

"You *did?*"

"Yeah. Something's wrong between Logan and me. I'm . . . just not always happy when I'm with him. I feel like he's taking over my life. I feel like I'm not Mary Anne anymore. I'm not whole. Logan *took* part of me."

"Did he *take* part of you, or did you *let* him take part of you?" Dawn asked wisely.

She is so smart.

"I guess I let him," I admitted. "I could have stood up for myself, but I didn't. I mean, I usually don't. Not really."

"So what are you going to do about this?"

My answer was ready. "I'm going to call Logan — now — and tell him we have to cool things for awhile. I need the time apart from him to think. Then when we've gotten ourselves together, we can pick up our relationship again. It will be hard to do, but I think it will be good for us."

"Whoa," said Dawn. "I never thought I'd hear you say that. Somehow I pictured you and Logan going steady through high school, then college, and finally getting married. After that, you'd have two children. Well, two or three. And — "

"Dawn!" I exclaimed. "Stop! First of all, I just want some time apart, not a break-up.

Second, I'm only thirteen. And Logan is the first boy I've ever been serious about. Did you really think we were going to get married?"

"Yes. And I'd be your maid of honor . . . wouldn't I?"

"I don't know. Yes. I mean, I hadn't exactly planned our wedding. I was planning on graduating from eighth grade first."

Dawn smiled. Then she stood up. "I'll leave you alone so you can call Logan," she said. "Use the phone in Mom and your father's room. For privacy. I'll be in my bedroom if you need me."

"Okay." I felt shaky. Dawn left, and I went into Dad and Sharon's room. I closed the door. Right away I thought, I could stop now if I wanted to. I don't *have* to call Logan.

But I called him anyway. Without even hesitating. I just picked up the receiver and punched the buttons.

Logan answered the phone. "Hi!" he said, when he heard my voice. He probably thought I was calling to apologize. He sounded as if he would accept my apology.

"Logan," I began, "this isn't going to be easy for me to say, but I'm calling — "

"To apologize, right?"

"Well, not really," I told him. "I'm calling

because I think we need to cool our relationship a little. I think — "

Logan interrupted me again. "Cool our relationship? *Why?*"

"I'm going to tell you, if you'll, um, if you'll just let me talk."

"All right, all right."

"I think we've been seeing too much of each other," I said. "I feel like you're — you're overtaking my life. You plan everything for us. You always want to be with me — and I *do* like being with you — but, I don't know. I guess I feel like you don't understand me very well anymore. . . ." I trailed off.

There was a pause. Then Logan said, "Okay," in an odd-sounding voice.

"Let's try cooling things for a few weeks," I went on, my voice beginning to quiver. (I just could not believe what I was doing.) "Then when we've had some time apart, we'll pick things up again."

"Okay."

"Well . . . good-bye."

"Good-bye. Good night," said Logan.

I hung up the phone. Then I burst into tears. I cried for a long time.

CHAPTER 7

Clangs, bangs, shouts.

It was Monday. Another week at Stoney-brook Middle School was beginning. I wondered what would happen that day. It was the first time I'd have the chance to see Logan since I'd called him and told him we needed to cool our relationship.

Would he respect what I'd said? Or would he be waiting at my locker like he usually was, but this time full of apologies and questions?

I approached my locker hesitantly.

"Mary Anne?" asked Dawn, who was walking with me. "Are you okay? You look funny. Kind of faraway."

"I was thinking about — " And at that moment I saw him.

Logan.

He was striding down the hall toward me. My locker was in between us. So he was going to wait for me after all.

Logan and I drew closer and closer and . . .

Logan walked right by Dawn and me. He didn't smile or say hello. He didn't even look at us. That was painful. But I told myself that what I was doing was meant to save our relationship.

"Mary Anne? Are you okay?" Dawn asked again.

"Yeah," I replied.

"Logan just ignored us."

"I know. I guess I told him to."

Dawn gave me a rueful smile, then left.

I spun the dial on my locker. I half expected to see a note stuck through the vent at the top of the door. Logan and I were always leaving notes for each other that way. Maybe Logan had gotten to school early, stuck a note in my locker, and then avoided looking at me because he knew he shouldn't have done that.

But there was no note.

That morning we had an assembly. I think it was about our school's dress code, but I wasn't paying much attention. Logan was sitting one row in front of me and four seats down. I had a perfect view of him. And if he turned his head slightly to the left, he had a pretty good view of me, too.

But we only glanced at each other once. And that was just because somebody near us dropped a book on the floor. As we looked around to see what had happened, our eyes met. Then we both faced front again.

Needless to say, Logan didn't sit with Dawn, Kristy, Stacey, Claudia, and me at lunch that day. (Jessi and Mal eat during another period, since they're in a different grade.) Not that Logan *al*ways sits at our table, but he usually does. And for the past several weeks he hadn't missed a day. He would move as close to me as he could get without actually sitting in my food. Sometimes he would feed me tidbits of his lunch, which was romantic, but embarrassing.

Anyway, the five of us sat at our usual table that Monday. When we had gotten settled, Kristy looked around. The first thing she said was, "Where's Logan, Mary Anne? Shouldn't he be in your lap?"

"He does not," I replied testily, "sit in my lap."

"*Sorry*," said Kristy. "But really. Where is he? In the library or someplace?"

I glanced at Dawn. She was the only one who knew what was going on between Logan and me. I knew I would tell the rest of my friends soon, because we don't usually keep secrets from each other. But I didn't feel like telling them right now.

"Oh, Logan's off with the guys," I said to Kristy. "He needs guy-talk, a break from us girls." I scanned the cafeteria. "See? There he is with Pete and Austin and Trevor and everyone."

Nobody questioned this. We ate, we talked about how bad the food was, we wondered how Jenny Prezzioso would react when the baby was born. Then lunch was over.

Whew.

By the end of the day, I felt drained. But working out relationships, I told myself, is not easy.

As I approached my locker after the last bell that afternoon, I could see Logan waiting for me. At least, I assumed he was at my locker. It was hard to tell since both walls are lined with lockers.

I began to walk more slowly. What was I going to say to Logan? What was he going to say to me? Maybe he'd thought things over and had decided we should break up. Noooo. I didn't want that.

When I finally reached my locker, feeling as if I were walking underwater, I dared to look into Logan's eyes. He looked into mine.

"I just wanted to say hi," he said seriously.

"Oh. Hi," I replied.

"See ya," said Logan, and walked off.

I stared after him. Well, that was better. We were speaking to each other, and I'd been expecting to do that. I do not consider the silent treatment to be a form of cooling off.

At home that night while Dawn and I were supposed to be doing our homework, I couldn't concentrate on anything — except Logan. In my history book, William Penn's face turned into Logan's. The romance story in our English text turned into a story about Logan and me.

"This is ridiculous," I said aloud.

"Mary Anne?" called Dawn from her room.

"Yeah? Can I come in? I need to talk."

"Sure. I'm ready for a break."

I walked down the hall, into Dawn's room, and sat on her bed. Dawn turned around in her desk chair.

"It's Logan, isn't it." she said. (It was a statement, not a question.)

I nodded.

"Are you having second thoughts about what you said to him?"

"I don't know. I can't stop thinking about him, about us."

"You did what you thought was right," Dawn told me. "You stood up for yourself."

"I guess . . ."

"Mary *Anne*," said Dawn, "remember how you've been feeling lately — like Logan's too pushy, always taking charge, not listening to you? You don't want to go back to that again, do you?"

"No. But I miss Logan."

"My mom missed my dad at first, right after the divorce. But she knew she'd done the right thing."

"I wish," I said, "that 'cooling off' didn't hurt so much."

CHAPTER 8

Tuesday

I sat for Jenny P. today. She's going through a rough time with this new baby business. You guys should know two things about Jenny right now: 1. She knows exactly what her mother is doing (bribing her) to make her feel good about the baby. 2. Jenny does NOT want to be a big sister. She wants to stay an only child. (Well, she didn't exactly say that, but that's what she meant.) I had a talk with her about brothers and sisters, but I'm not sure how much she got out of it.

Who could be a better expert on brothers and sisters than Mallory? She has more of them than any other member of the BSC. (Although Kristy comes close, having six.) So I was glad that Mal had at least one sitting job with Jenny before the baby was born.

Mrs. Prezzioso left Jenny and Mal at about four o'clock to go to a lecture on childbirth at the hospital. Just like when I had sat for Jenny, the first thing she did after her mother left was take Mal's hand and say, "Want to come up to my room and see my new stuff from Mommy?"

More new stuff? I wondered as I read Mal's notebook entry. Or was it the same new stuff she'd shown me?

Nope. It was *more* new stuff.

"See? Mommy got me this letters-and-numbers learning machine. Big girls have to start learning hard things because they'll be going to school soon. And she got me a workbook. Oh, and this doll. I'll tell you about the doll later. Want to see my new grown-up clothes?" Jenny went on.

"Sure," replied Mallory.

Jenny opened her closet door and pushed some coat hangers to one side. "Here's a new dress. Here's another new dress. And here is

69

a *very* grown-up outfit." Jenny pointed to a pink plaid jumper over a white cotton blouse. "And this hat" (a pink straw hat with a white ribbon around it), "and these shoes" (pink ballet slippers), "go with the outfit."

Mal nodded. "Beautiful," she said. She paused. Then she asked, "What were you going to tell me about your new doll?"

Jenny scowled. "The doll is different from the other new things. Mommy buys me those new things so I won't be mad about the baby. But the doll is for this. Come on." Jenny picked up the doll and left her room. Mal followed her. They walked down the hall to the room next to Jenny's.

"This is the baby's room," Jenny informed Mal.

"It's very pretty," said Mal politely, looking at the cheerful yellow-and-white room. A white rug covered the floor. Yellow-and-white striped curtains hung at the windows. The walls had been painted a pale, pale yellow, and around the walls ran a frieze of parading ducks and lambs. The Prezziosos were ready for the baby. The crib was made up (some stuffed animals already sat in it); the changing table was equipped with diapers, powder, Baby-Wipes, and more; and a yellow duck lamp sat on the dresser. Everything looked brand-new, except for the crib.

As if she had read Mal's mind, Jenny said, "That used to be *my* crib."

Mal wasn't sure what to say to that, but it didn't matter. Jenny didn't seem to expect an answer. She had marched over to the crib, expertly pulled the side down, and placed her new doll on the mattress.

"Mommy," said Jenny, "is teaching me to diaper my doll and give it a bottle."

"It?" repeated Mal. "Isn't your doll a girl or a boy?"

"Not yet," replied Jenny.

Mal let that one go by. She said, "Show me what you've learned so far."

"Okay," said Jenny grimly. She moved the doll from the crib to the changing table. Then, steadying the doll with one hand, she reached for a disposable diaper. And *then*, as if she'd done it a thousand times before, she cleaned her doll with a Baby-Wipe, shook some powder on it, and then peeled off the tabs on the diaper and fastened it securely to her "baby."

"Wow! Very nice," said Mal. "Soon you'll be ready to be a baby-sitter yourself. Maybe you can join the Baby-sitters Club."

Jenny didn't even crack a smile. "I'll be busy

with *our* baby," she said. "Anyway, look. See how you give a bottle to a baby?" Jenny sat in a rocking chair, held the doll carefully, and pretended to feed it. "Then you burp the baby," she went on. Jenny put the doll to her shoulder, patted its back, and said, "Burp!"

Mal smiled. "Terrific!"

"I told you I could do it. Mommy makes me practice every day."

"Oh."

With that, Jenny stood up, walked out of the baby's room, and down the hall toward hers. But instead of going into her room, she just tossed the doll through the doorway as she went by.

"Can we have a snack?" asked Jenny as she headed downstairs.

"Sure," said Mal. "Let's make peanut butter crackers."

"Yum!" was Jenny's reply.

Mal got out paper plates, napkins, two plastic knives, a jar of peanut butter, and a box of crackers. Also a bottle of grape juice.

Jenny and Mal ate in silence at first. Then Mal asked, "So how do you feel about becoming a big girl?"

"I already am a big girl," replied Jenny.

Mal smiled. "That's true. You are a big girl.

I guess I meant how does it feel to know you're going to be a big sister?"

"Yucky." Jenny was spreading peanut butter on a cracker. She didn't look at Mal.

"Yucky? How come?"

"Because of what I just showed you. The baby is going to need lots of help. Mommy and Daddy will probably spend all their time with the baby. The baby won't know how to feed itself or anything. Mommy will have to feed it, and carry it places, and change its diapers, and — I don't know. Lots of things."

"But," said Mal, trying to create a bright spot in what Jenny saw as her dark future, "babies sleep a lot. You'll be able to spend plenty of time with your mom and dad when the baby's asleep."

"I guess . . ."

"You know, I have *seven* brothers and sisters," Mal pointed out.

"I know. I'm sorry."

"No, it's great!" exclaimed Mal.

"How can it be?"

"For lots of reasons. There's always somebody around to talk to or play with. Plus, I *like* taking care of my younger brothers and sisters. I feel grown-up and important. I can teach them things. *And* — guess what being the oldest means."

"What?" asked Jenny.

"It means you get to do things first. I'm the only girl in my family with pierced ears. Vanessa and Margo and Claire will have to wait a few years before they get theirs pierced."

Jenny looked interested.

"Plus, think of all the things you can do that the baby *won't* be able to do. You can ride your tricycle. You can play games. You can look at books. You can go into the backyard to swing and slide. The baby won't be able to do that. The baby will be stuck, depending on your mom or dad to carry it around."

"Plus, I can talk," added Jenny.

"That's right," said Mal. "You can say, 'Mommy, I'm hungry.' Or, 'Mommy, I'm tired.' When the baby wants something, all it will be able to do is cry. Then your parents will have to *guess* what it wants."

Jenny was silent for moment. Finally she said, "Mallory? Do you *really* like having brothers and sisters?"

"I really do. When they're babies, I can take care of them. When they grow up, they become my friends. I'm never lonely."

"After the baby, you and I will be kind of alike," said Jenny.

"We will?" Mal asked.

"Yup. We'll both be the oldest in our families. And we're both girls."

"That's right!" said Mal. "Maybe we should form a Big Sisters Club."

Jenny smiled this time, but she didn't look deliriously happy. In fact, her smile faded and she stared into space, saying nothing.

"Jenny? What are you thinking about?" Mal wanted to know.

Jenny sighed. "Oh, the baby. I know I'll be able to do more stuff and have more fun than the baby. But some things are going to change."

"That's true," Mal agreed.

"I'm used to having Mommy and Daddy all to me. Now I won't be so important. The baby will be here, and it will be important, too."

"Oh, Jen," said Mal, suddenly feeling sympathetic. "You'll be just as important as you were before."

Jenny looked unconvinced. And Mal thought she knew why. Mal didn't remember ever having been the only child. She was just a year old when the triplets were born. But Jenny had been the center of attention for *four years*. Now she was going to lose that position.

It would be hard for anybody.

CHAPTER 9

"Mary Anne! You look — " Kristy started to say something, but thought better of it. For once, she controlled her big mouth.

I had a pretty good idea how I looked, though: awful. It was a Monday afternoon, just before a club meeting, so my friends had seen me in school a few hours earlier. I hadn't looked great then (I hadn't been sleeping well), but I couldn't possibly have looked as horrible as I did by 5:20. That was because I'd spent most of the afternoon crying. I'd been home alone. (Dad and Sharon were at work; Dawn was baby-sitting.) And I'd been thinking about what Logan and I were going through. I'd started to cry and couldn't stop. Now my nose was red and my face was blotchy, plus I had dark circles under my eyes.

"I know," I said to Kristy. "I look like my own evil twin."

Kristy laughed. "You don't look *that* bad.

But something is wrong, isn't it, Mary Anne? Are you in trouble?"

I shook my head.

"Do you want to talk about it?"

"Not yet," I replied. "We might as well wait until everyone else gets here. Then I won't have to tell the story five times."

"Okay." Kristy settled herself in the director's chair and adjusted her visor. She was ready for the meeting.

I sat on Claud's bed.

We waited.

By five-thirty, everyone had arrived, and Kristy called our meeting to order. We got club business out of the way, and then waited for the phone to ring. When it didn't, Kristy looked at me with raised eyebrows. The others then glanced from Kristy to me. I could almost hear them wondering what was going on.

I cleared my throat. "Um, you guys have noticed that Logan hasn't been sitting at our lunch table recently."

My friends nodded curiously, except for Dawn, who knew the story already. And Stacey said, "You haven't exactly been yourself, either."

"I know," I replied. "Well, the thing is, I told Logan that I wanted to cool our relationship a little." I looked down at my shoes. "I didn't know how hard that would be, but I *had* to do it. See, Logan was getting to be — I mean, I felt like he was taking over my life. Or taking something away from it. So I told him I wanted to cool things off, and well, we haven't spoken in days."

"I noticed that he hasn't been hanging around your locker," said Kristy.

I nodded. "He hasn't called or anything. When I said 'cool off' I didn't mean 'break up,' but I think Logan took it that way."

Jessi gasped.

"What is it? What's wrong?" asked the rest of us.

"I can't believe you guys are breaking up. It seems like you've been a couple practically forever," said Jessi.

"*I* thought they were going to *be* a couple forever," said Dawn. "I thought they'd go through school together, then get married, then have kids — "

Dawn stopped talking when Stacey cleared her throat loudly.

I was crying. As usual.

"Oh, Mary Anne, I'm sorry," said Dawn, leaning over to give me a hug.

"That's okay. Almost anything makes me cry these days." I sniffed.

The phone rang then, and we arranged for a sitter at the Perkinses'.

When business was over, Stacey said quietly, "Separation is never easy. Remember when I thought I was in love with that lifeguard? Boy, was I hurt when I found out he had a girlfriend."

"But then Toby came along," Mary Anne reminded me.

"And then we had to separate when vacation was over and we left the beach."

"And I had to separate from Alex, Toby's cousin, remember? That hurt, too."

"But then *Logan* came along."

"And now we're . . ."

I couldn't finish my sentence, so Claudia said, "Well, I fell in love with Will at camp, and then we had to leave each other when camp was over. And then I fell in love with Terry in California, and *we* had to separate."

"Ow, ow, ow!" said Jessi. (We looked at her as if she were crazy.) "All this separating," she explained. "All this hurting. Ouch!"

We laughed. Then Claudia continued, "I fell in love when we were on the cruise through the Bahamas. How come we always fall in love when we're out of town and the relationship can't last?"

"Logan's in town," I said.

"And maybe your relationship *will* last," Mal pointed out.

"I hope so."

I looked around the room then at all the somber faces, and was glad when the phone rang again. We needed something to lighten the atmosphere.

And the call certainly did lighten the atmosphere. That was because the caller was Karen, Kristy's little stepsister. "Just a sec," said Dawn, who'd answered the phone. "I'll turn you over to Kristy."

Dawn handed the phone to our president, whispering, "It's Karen."

Kristy smiled. "Hi, Karen. What's up? . . . You want to hire a baby-sitter?"

My friends and I looked at each other, amused. We were even more amused to hear Kristy say, as gently as possible, "We don't usually sit for stuffed animals. Haven't Moosie and Goosie stayed by themselves lots of times before?" (Moosie and Goosie are identical stuffed cats. Karen keeps Moosie at her father's house, and Goosie at her mother's house.) There was a pause. Then, "Why don't you introduce them to some of Andrew's animals?" we heard Kristy suggest.

Kristy and Karen talked for a few more minutes before hanging up the phone. When the receiver was back in its cradle, Kristy burst out laughing. "Can you believe it?" she asked. "Karen suddenly decided that Moosie and Goosie get lonely when they're home alone. So she wanted to hire us as sitters. She offered to pay us fifteen cents an hour."

The rest of us couldn't help giggling.

"I suggested that she introduce them to some other stuffed animals," Kristy continued.

"That was nice," said Jessi, grinning.

"Thanks," said Kristy. "I try to be sensitive to Karen and Andrew. They've been through separations like the rest of us — and they're a lot younger."

Another job call and then another came in. When we were finished handling them, I said, "You know what? I don't know if Jenny realizes it, but in a way she's anticipating a separation from her parents when the baby comes. She knows she won't be the center of attention anymore."

"Poor Jenny," said Kristy sincerely. (Generally, Kristy doesn't like Jenny.)

Something occurred to me then. "Hey, you guys," I said, "I just thought of something. Okay, so we've been talking about all these separations. But you know what the difference is with Logan and me? I'm *choosing* to leave him. He isn't leaving me. In a way, I have control over this situation. I can — "

The phone rang, and this time I answered it. Guess who was calling?

"Logan?" I exclaimed.

"Hi," he said. "I've got business to discuss with you." (He *did* sound businesslike.) "I need a sitter for Kerry and Hunter" (they're Logan's younger sister and brother), "on Valentine's Day. It's a Friday night. Mom and Dad are going out, and now so am I. Kerry and Hunter asked if you'd be their sitter, Mary Anne. I know that's not club policy, but they miss you."

"I'll get back to you," I told him brusquely, and hung up the phone.

I looked at my friends in shock and amazement, and told them what Logan had just told me. Everybody was saying, "Go ahead and take the job," or things like that, but all I could think was, Who was Logan going out with on Valentine's Day? Had he found another girlfriend? And did I really want to go over there and see him leave the house with some new girl?

But then I remembered Logan saying that Hunter and Kerry missed me. I didn't want to disappoint them. Besides, as a professional businesswoman, I shouldn't let emotions get in the way of my job.

So I called Logan back and told him that I would sit that night.

"Great," he said. "Thanks, Mary Anne."

"You're welcome."

"See ya."

"See ya. . . . 'Bye."

I tried to imagine Logan's girlfriend. She was probably the opposite of me — tall, blonde, not shy, self-assured. Maybe *that* was what had gone wrong in our relationship. I was so shy that Logan felt he *had* to take over for me.

Oh, well. I began to look forward to Valentine's Day in the same way I look forward to a trip to the dentist.

CHAPTER 10

"Da-da. Ma-ma. Goo-goo."

I closed my eyes for a moment. Jenny was giving me a headache. It was a Saturday evening, and I was taking care of her from six until ten. And she was pretending she was a baby. She was driving me crazy.

I looked at my watch. It was only 6:45.

I sighed. Not only was Jenny driving me crazy, but I was driving myself crazy. I couldn't stop thinking about Logan. I kept imagining his new girlfriend. But that was all I *could* do — imagine. I hadn't seen him with the girlfriend yet. Not in school, not downtown, not anywhere.

So my imagination was running wild. Now not only was the girl tall, blonde, not shy, and very self-assured, but she was *extremely* smart; had a lovely, romantic name like Olivia; and was getting started in a promising singing career. Sometimes Logan would go to the sound studios with her. Maybe one day he would be "discovered" at the studios. (He *is* awfully handsome). Then he would become an actor and, after college, he and Olivia would go to Hollywood and make it big.

"Ma-ma," said Jenny again. She patted my knee. She'd been crawling around the living room, but now she was sitting on the floor, sucking her thumb.

"Yes, Jenny?" I said. (I was low on patience.)

"Not Jenny! Baby. Me baby."

"Okay, baby. What do you want?" I tried to concentrate on her instead of on Logan and Olivia.

"Wet. Baby wet." When I didn't respond right away (I mean, what was I supposed to say?), Jenny tugged on my jeans. "BABY WET!" she screamed. "DIAPER!"

"Okay." I pretended to reach for a diaper, then fasten it on Jenny.

"NO! Real diaper."

"Jenny, I'm not going to put a diaper on you," I said. "That's silly."

Jenny got to her hands and knees again, and crawled frantically out of the living room. I could hear her going upstairs. A few minutes later she crawled back to me (I was daydreaming about Logan again) with a diaper in her mouth.

"Put diaper on baby," she demanded.

You do *not* need a diaper," I replied. "You're a big girl. You can use the bathroom now."

"NO! Not a big girl. Me baby."

"I know. You already told me."

"PUT DIAPER ON!"

"Jenny," I said with as much patience as I could muster, "I am not going to put a diaper on you."

"Okay-ay," said Jenny, switching to a sing-song, four-year-old voice.

"Thank you," I replied, not realizing that I should have paid more attention to that change in her voice. "Now would you please go back to the baby's room and put the diaper where it belongs?"

"Okay-ay," said Jenny again.

She stood up and marched out of the room. And I went back to Logan and Olivia. They were living in Hollywood with a mansion and a swimming pool and maybe a tennis court. Once or twice a month, Olivia would throw a huge, gala party for their glamorous friends, and Logan would often say to her, "What a wonderful hostess you are, dear. Mary Anne could never have done anything like this."

It was at that point that I heard a thump from upstairs. I realized that Jenny should have been back long ago from returning the diaper. What was I doing? Certainly not being a responsible baby-sitter, I thought, as I dashed up the stairs.

"Jenny?" I called.

No answer.

I peeked into her room. It was neat . . . and empty.

So I ran down the hall to the baby's room.

I could not believe what I saw.

It was an absolute wreck. Everything on the changing table had been swept off and was scattered across the floor. Everything in the crib had been thrown out. Stuffed animals and bedding had been flung from one side of the room to the other. The drawers in the dresser had been opened and clothing was draped over the animals and diapers. Jenny was now attempting to scale the dresser — I guess in hopes of attacking the yellow duck lamp.

She had trashed the baby's room.

"Hold it!" I cried.

Jenny stumbled and fell to the floor. But she didn't cry. She had landed on diapers and a pile of clothes.

"What on earth do you think you're doing?" I demanded.

"I hate the baby," was Jenny's reply.

"Well, I'm sorry, kiddo," I said, "but the baby is coming whether you like it or not. And whether you mess up the room or not. There are going to be some things in life" (Oh, no, I sounded like my father!) "that you can't change. The baby is one of them. Now I want this room cleaned up *right away*."

Jenny looked at me, eyes as big as basketballs. (I guess I'd never spoken to her in that tone of voice.) Then, wordlessly, she began to put things back in the crib, on the changing table, in the dresser.

I helped her, especially with the clothes. Jenny was not a very good folder yet. And as we worked (in silence) I got an idea.

When the room looked the way it should (the way I remembered it looking), I turned to Jenny and said, "Okay, baby. What about a bottle?"

Jenny's face changed from sullen to surprised and then to pleased. "Me baby?"

"Yes, you baby. Let's go downstairs. I'll fix you something to drink before bedtime. How's that?"

"Da-da-da-da-da-da!" exclaimed Jenny. She crawled out of the baby's room and followed me down the hall. When we reached the top of the steps, I bent over and scooped Jenny into my arms.

"Hey!" she cried. "What are you doing?"

"I'm carrying you downstairs."

"But I can go down myself."

"Not if you're a baby," I told her. "You might fall."

"Oh."

I carried Jenny all the way into the kitchen and sat her in the high chair that the Prezziosos had been storing in their basement, but which now stood off in a corner of the kitchen.

"Hey!" said Jenny again. "I can't fit in here."

But she could, even though it was a tight squeeze. And I said, "This is where babies eat. And you're a baby, remember?"

"Yeah . . ." said Jenny slowly.

"All right. Now I'll fix you something nice to drink." I took a carton of milk out of the refrigerator and started to pour it into a pan.

"What's that?" Jenny called from the high chair.

"Milk," I told her.

"I don't like milk. I want juice."

"But babies drink milk. . . . And they drink it warm."

Jenny practically gagged at the idea of warm

89

milk. Then she said, "I don't want a drink after all. I mean — Da-da-da. No milk for baby."

She had caught me just before I poured the milk into the pan. "Are you sure?" I asked her. "Because it's almost bedtime."

"No it isn't. I get to stay up lots later than this."

"Babies don't," I reminded her. "They need tons of sleep. They go to bed right after supper and don't get up until the morning. Unless they're hungry and need another bottle of warm milk in the middle of the night."

Jenny appeared stumped. Clearly, the "game" was not going the way she wanted. She tried another tactic. "Baby hungry. Want snack."

"Oh. Okay," I replied. I found the cereal and plopped a handful of Cheerios onto the tray of the high chair.

Jenny glanced from the cereal to me. "Want Oreos," she said.

"Not for babies." (How many times had I said that in the last ten minutes?)

"Not for babies?" repeated Jenny.

"No way. Babies can't eat Oreos."

Again, Jenny looked stumped. Finally she said, "Goo-goo. No snack. Snack over." She tried to disengage herself from the high chair, but I lifted her out — and carried her toward the door.

"Where we go?" asked the baby Jenny.

"Nighty-night time," I replied.

"You mean I'm really going to bed?"

"Yes. In the crib."

"But I'm too big for the crib." Jenny paused. Then she said, "Mary Anne? I'm tired of this game. I don't want to be a baby anymore."

"Are you sure?" I asked her. "You're passing up all sorts of good things. Warm milk, a nice crib to sleep in . . ."

Jenny wriggled out of my arms. "I'm sure," she said. "I want to watch TV. And before I go to sleep tonight — *in my own bed* — I want juice and cookies."

"Okay," I replied. "Boy, it sure is nice to have Jenny back. You're much more fun than a baby."

Jenny smiled. "I feel sort of sorry for babies," she informed me.

CHAPTER 11

At 11:45 on a Saturday morning, the phone rang. Even though I'd been sitting by the phone for fifteen minutes, *waiting* for it to ring, I jumped. Then I picked up the receiver and, trying to sound calm, said, "Hello?"

"It's time," said a man's voice.

I couldn't control myself any longer. "You mean she just left? Great! I'll call Stacey and Claudia. We'll get there as soon as we can. See ya!" I depressed the button on the phone, then let it up and immediately dialed Claud's number. When she answered her phone, I said, "All clear! Go to the Prezziosos' right now!"

"Okay!" cried Claudia. "Stacey's here with me. We're ready to leave."

"Great. I'll see you in a few minutes."

It was the day of the baby shower for Mrs. Prezzioso. It was also about three days before

Mrs. P.'s birthday, so a friend had invited her to lunch in a fancy restaurant to celebrate. The lunch was just a ruse, though. The friend was getting Mrs. P. out of the house so that Stacey, Claudia, Mr. P., and I could prepare for the shower and surprise Mrs. P. when her friend brought her home.

Mr. P. had thought of everything. He'd told Mrs. P.'s friend to bring her back around one-thirty, no earlier. He'd invited the guests for one o'clock and told them to park their cars down the street so Mrs. P. wouldn't get suspicious. And anything he'd had to buy for the party he'd hidden in the attic.

I reached the Prezziosos' before Stacey and Claud did, since I live close by. But they showed up about ten minutes later — just in time for chaos. When I'd arrived, things had been relatively calm. I mean, relative to the way they became ten minutes later.

Jenny had answered the door, still in her pajamas. Mr. P. was right behind her. "Come in, come in!" he said, smiling. I stepped inside, took off my coat, and hung it in the closet. Mr. P. continued, "I think everything is in order. The cake is being delivered, I've gotten the stuff out of the attic, and the caterers are on their way with the food."

"Terrific," I said. I grinned at Jenny. "Are you excited? There's going to be a party here today."

"And Mary Anne is going to get you all dressed up," added her father.

"I don't want to get dressed up," said Jenny flatly.

"Well, I'm afraid you have to," Mr. P. said, not sounding quite so calm. "Mommy will want you dressed up."

Just when Jenny looked as if she were going to pitch a fit, the bell rang. I was sure it was Claudia and Stacey, so I opened the door. Standing on the stoop was a man from the bakery, carrying a large white box tied up with string.

"Mr. Prezzioso, it's the cake," I said.

"Oh, good." Mr. P. edged past me and held open the door for the delivery man. "The stork cake, right?" Mr. P. said. "With 'Congratulations' on it?"

The man shook his head. "Nope. What I got here is a pink flowery cake. Says 'Happy Birthday, Ginnie' on it."

He looked unconcerned, but I could see Mr. P. growing edgy.

"That's not our cake," said Jenny's father. "Ours is for a baby shower."

"Hm," said the man.

"Could you check your van?" asked Mr. P. "I specifically ordered a stork cake for noon today."

"All right-y." The man returned to his van.

While he did so, the phone rang. All I could hear of Mr. P's end of the conversation was groaning. When he got off the phone he said to me, "That was the catering service. They're going to be late with the food. But they promised to be here between one and one-fifteen. That's cutting it close. . . . Oh, I *knew* things were going too well this morning."

And that's when Claud and Stacey arrived — with Jenny whining and complaining, the delivery man searching through his truck, and Mr. P. going crazy over the caterers.

But things began to change. The delivery man found the right cake. Stacey and Claudia took over the decorating and set up the food table. And I managed to get Jenny upstairs.

"Look," I said. "Your father laid out some clothes for you to wear."

"It's one of my new grown-up outfits," replied Jenny. (It was the pink jumper and hat ensemble she'd shown Mallory.)

"Well, it's lovely. Okay. Out of your pajamas."

"No."

"Yes. Out of your pajamas and into those clothes."

Jenny didn't reply, but she made a face. And then she refused to take off her pajamas or put on the new outfit, so I had to do everything for her.

"I don't see why I have to get dressed up," she said. "The party is for the baby, not me. People are going to bring presents and they'll all be for that darn old baby."

"That darn old baby is going to be your brother or sister, remember?"

"Yes. . . . OW!"

I was brushing Jenny's hair, but I hadn't hit so much as a tiny snarl.

"Do you want to wear some of your jewelry?" I asked, when her hair had been thoroughly brushed and was shining.

"No."

And that was that.

Jewelry or not, Mr. P. thought Jenny looked fine — when I finally got her back down the stairs. She balked, complained, and thought of excuses for staying in her room, every step of the way.

"Hey, Jenny!" I said. "Look at the living room. Look what Claud and Stacey have done to it."

They had transformed it. I think Jenny was impressed, but she didn't want to let on. *I* let on, however. "This is beautiful, you guys!" I exclaimed. The room was like a pastel cloud. Pale pink, blue, and yellow streamers lazily criss-crossed the ceiling. Bunches of balloons had been fastened here and there. On the food table was an airy yellow tablecloth, bouquets of flowers, and a huge fold-out stork carrying a bundle in its beak. Out of the bundle peeked a doll's face.

Jenny looked at the stork intently. "What is that bird doing?" she asked.

I tried to explain.

"You mean storks bring babies?"

"Well, no — " Stacey began to say.

But Jenny wasn't paying attention. " 'Cause if *that's* true," she went on, "I'll just make a big sign for our roof, and it will say, 'DO NOT LEAVE ANY BABIES HERE. EVER.' "

Stacey and Claudia and I looked at each other helplessly. Finally Claudia said, "I don't think that will work. You know how fat your mommy's tummy has gotten? Well, that's because the baby is — "

"I think Jenny should discuss this with her parents," I interrupted. Then, to distract Jenny, I said, "Hey, look how Claudia decorated that cradle. That's where all the presents will go." I indicated the crepe paper and flowers that adorned the cradle.

Jenny narrowed her eyes. "The presents are going in *there?* That used to be *my* cradle. When I was a baby."

"I give up," I whispered to Stacey and Claudia.

Luckily, things started to happen then. The first guests arrived, along with the catered food. Mr. P. talked to the guests, while my friends and I arranged the food on the table. Almost before I knew it, Mr. P. was looking around and announcing, "Everyone's here. And our guest of honor should be back in about five minutes."

The guests hid themselves in the dining room and kitchen. I pulled Jenny behind an armchair and said, "Shh."

"Why are we hiding and whispering?" she asked me.

"Because any second now your mommy is going to walk through the front door, and everyone is going to jump out and say 'Surprise!' "

Jenny looked interested, at least. And when the door did open and her mother did step into the living room, Jenny was the first to jump out.

Mrs. P. was properly surprised. I mean,

really surprised. For a second, her mouth just formed an O. Then she buried her face in her hands and laughed, cried, and blushed, all at the same time, as her friends surrounded her. When she composed herself, Mr. P. led her to a chair next to the cradle. And then the fun began.

Mrs. P. reached into the cradle and pulled out a gift. "From Margery," she read. "Thank you!"

The woman named Margery dug around in her purse and unearthed a smaller package. "I didn't forget the new big sister!" she exclaimed, and handed the present to Jenny.

"For *me?*" Jenny beamed. She opened her small present while her mother opened a much larger one. The larger one turned out to be an acute stuffed teddy bear. Jenny's gift was a pair of plastic barrettes. She couldn't hide her disappointment. And didn't even try to, as guest after guest handed her some small item while her mother opened much more elaborate gifts for the baby.

"Jenny, you could at least say thank you," I whispered to her.

Jenny did not answer me. I decided that teaching her manners was not part of my baby-sitting job. So I sat back and enjoyed the rest of the shower. (Later, Stacey and Claudia and

I agreed that the shower had been fun, but that if we ever heard another person say, "Oh, isn't that *cute?*" we'd barf.)

At last the guests began to leave. When everyone had gone, my friends and I walked around with garbage bags, stuffing them with crumpled, lipstick-stained paper napkins; empty cups; bits of crepe paper; scraps of food; and a mountain of wrapping paper.

"So, Jenny," I said. "What did you think of the party?"

Jenny looked at her little pile of gifts. "Yucky," she said.

"But all those people brought you presents," Claudia pointed out.

"The baby got better ones."

I glanced at Mrs. P., still sitting in her chair, but she was engrossed in a baby book she'd been given.

"Jenny — " I started to say.

Jenny interrupted me. "You know what? I HATE THAT BABY!"

CHAPTER 12

The following Friday was Valentine's Day. At breakfast, Dad, Sharon, Dawn, and I exchanged silly cards. We laughed, but I had to force myself to keep from thinking about Logan. Here it was, the most romantic day of the year, and we probably wouldn't even speak to each other. A few days earlier I'd been in a stationery store and had seen the perfect card for Logan. It was huge, and cost a lot of money for a card. I didn't buy it. Not because it was too expensive, but because there was no point. I cried a little, right there in the store. By Valentine's Day I felt better. It was impossible not to, what with the funny cards, and Sharon putting red food coloring in the butter so we could have a pink spread on our toast.

And after school, the BSC held a small party before the Friday meeting.

"Red hots!" Claud announced. "I've got red

101

hots and heart candies and even . . . chocolate-covered cherries!"

It was a sugar-fest (although Claud had thoughtfully provided pretzels for Stacey and Dawn, our noncandy eaters).

We lolled around and talked about school and friends. We giggled. Stacey was in the process of painting everyone's fingernails red when Kristy suddenly announced, "Okay! Come to order! It's time to start the meeting."

Automatically, I checked Claud's digital clock. It read 5:30 on the nose. I couldn't believe it. During the entire party, Kristy had been clock-watching.

Oh, well. That's Kristy for you.

The meeting went by quickly. At six o'clock, as we were getting ready to leave, I said to Dawn, "Remind Dad and your mom that I won't be home until around ten tonight, okay?"

"Oh, that's right," Dawn replied. "You'll be at Logan's, sitting for Kerry and Hunter." She paused, then added, "How do you feel about that?"

"I don't know," I said honestly. "I mean, I like Kerry and Hunter, and I'm flattered that they specifically asked for *me* to be their sitter. But I don't know if I can face seeing Logan and Olivia leave the house on their date."

"Who's Olivia?" asked Dawn, Jessi, Kristy, Stacey, Mal, and Claud.

I realized two things then: that everyone had been listening to my conversation with Dawn, and that the nonexistent Olivia had become real to me. Did that mean I was cracking up?

My friends were waiting for an answer, so I mumbled something and then dashed out of Claud's room. Behind me I could hear Stacey saying, "What? His cousin?" and Mallory saying, "I think she said, 'No one.' "

Anyway, I walked quickly to Logan's house. The evening was cold, so I stuffed my hands in my pockets. I was glad I was wearing jeans and an old ski sweater under my parka. I didn't look glamorous, but I was warm.

A few minutes later, I reached the Brunos'. (I could have found my way there blindfolded.) I stood on the stoop, reached up to press the doorbell — and froze. My finger wouldn't move. I was too afraid of what I'd find in there. Logan and his girlfriend ready for their date? Mrs. Bruno taking pictures of them?

Oh, well. I had to be an adult about this. I forced myself to ring the bell.

Instead of running footsteps, I heard nothing. Silence. I noticed that the Brunos' house looked pretty dark. Had I gotten my dates mixed up? No, Logan had definitely said Valentine's Day, and this was Valentine's Day. Wrong house? No way.

Just as I was wondering what could possibly be wrong — and just as I was growing a teeny bit scared — the front door creaked open. Shadowed against a dim light from the kitchen down the hall stood Logan. He was wearing a tux and holding a box containing a wrist corsage.

Oh, this was just too much. A wrist corsage (an orchid) for Olivia? I half expected Logan to say, "Oh, it's just you," and to look over my shoulder to see if Olivia was arriving yet.

Instead, Logan smiled slowly and shyly at me. "Hi, Mary Anne," he said. Then he added, "Happy Valentine's Day."

"Hi, Logan," I replied.

"Come on in."

Logan held the door open for me, and I slipped past him, into the hallway. "Where are Hunter and Kerry?" I asked as I took off my jacket. "I've never heard your house this quiet."

"Oh, they're here," Logan told me. "They're down in the rec room with Mom and Dad. I made them promise to stay there all evening."

"I thought your parents were going out to-night," I said, puzzled and somewhat apprehensive. "That's why I — "

Logan interrupted me by putting his finger to my lips. "Shh," he said. "Come see." He took my hand and led me to the dining room. There I saw the table set for a romantic dinner for two. Candles burned in silver holders. A white cloth covered the table. The Brunos' best china gleamed next to crystal glasses and sparkling silverware.

Torture.

Logan was making me see how he and Olivia were going to spend Valentine's Day evening. How low could a person get?

I was about to say something when Logan spoke up first. "Surprise," he said softly. He opened the box and slipped the corsage onto my wrist.

"Huh?" I asked brightly.

"This is for *us*, Mary Anne. You're not here to baby-sit. That was . . . well, it was a trick. It was the only way I could give you this present, this evening. Anyway, like I said, everyone's in the rec room. They won't bother us. Tonight is our night."

My jaw dropped open. "I thought we were going to cool our — "

"We did," said Logan. "And now I'm ready to try warming it up again. Here, have a seat. My family helped me make this special dinner just for us."

I was completely overwhelmed. So I sat down. I think that if Logan had said (as gently and as sweetly as he had spoken just now), "Here. Shave your head, get each of your ears pierced four times and your nose once, and go be a sheepherder in the mountains," I would have done it.

"Are you hungry?" Logan asked. He was standing at my elbow, like a waiter.

"Yes," I admitted.

"Good. We'll be eating soon. But first I have some things for you. Just a minute. Stay right here."

Logan disappeared into the kitchen, swinging the door shut behind him. When he returned, his arms were loaded. Grinning, he set a small gift-wrapped package by my plate, and then a red heart-shaped box. After that, he handed me a single red rose. "For you," he said.

"But you already gave me a flower," I replied, looking at the orchid on my wrist. I was completely bewildered.

"Red roses are traditional on Valentine's Day."

I wasn't sure what to do with the rose (its stem was *very* long; also thorny), so I just laid it next to my plate on the white tablecloth.

Logan was nudging the present and the heart-shaped box closer to me. (He still hadn't sat down.) "Go ahead. Open them," he said.

"Only if you'll sit down, too," I said with a nervous smile. I just could not believe what was going on. It had happened too fast. I was supposed to be baby-sitting, but here I was in a candlelit room, a world of romance. And Logan, all dressed up, was presenting me with gift after gift, while I sat dumbfounded, feeling guilty because I hadn't even bought Logan that card I'd seen.

Logan sat. I looked at the boxes in front of me. "Which one first?" I asked.

"Mmm . . . that one." Logan pointed to the heart-shaped box.

In all honesty, I must say that the box was pretty gaudy. It was adorned with a gigantic pink plastic rose and tied with red voile. (Or toile. Whatever that stuff wedding veils are made of.)

I slipped off the voile or toile. Inside the box were five pounds of chocolate candy. "Yum," I said. "Thanks, Logan."

"Any time. Let's save them for dessert. Open the other present."

I reached for the small silver-wrapped box and unwrapped it. When I lifted the lid I saw . . . a bracelet made of tiny gold hearts linked together.

I gasped. And Logan leaned over and kissed my cheek.

At that moment I still felt overwhelmed. But I felt something new, too. It was a gnawing sense of dread.

I was in over my head with Logan. This was not at all the way things were supposed to be working. And I didn't know what to do, how to fix them.

"Logan, this is beautiful," I ventured.

"I knew you'd like it," was Logan's answer. He fastened it around my wrist.

It really was beautiful — but now I had to say sheepishly, "Logan, I didn't get anything for you. I saw this card, but . . ." My voice trailed off.

"That's okay," he said. "Eating dinner with you is enough of a gift."

I wanted to cry.

Logan went back into the kitchen then, and returned carrying two plates of food — lasagna, broccoli with some sort of sauce on it, and a serving of salad.

"Wow!" I couldn't help being impressed.

"Just remember," said Logan, as he set one of the plates in front of me, "I had a little help with this."

"And now you're forcing your family to spend the evening in the rec room?"

"Under penalty of death," replied Logan.

We began to eat. For awhile, we ate in silence. When the silence became excruciating, I said, "Logan, I feel *really* bad that I don't have anything for you. You've given me flowers, candy, a bracelet, and dinner."

"Don't worry about it. I've been planning this as a surprise. How could you have known about it?"

I just shook my head.

We made it through dinner. We made it through dessert (chocolate cake and chocolate candy — Claudia would have been in heaven). As soon as dessert was over, I looked at my watch.

"Logan, I better go," I said.

"Okay, I'll ask Mom or Dad to drive us to your house."

"Wait! Before we leave I have to say something." My heart was pounding but I was determined to speak up. "Logan — Logan, when I said we should cool our relationship, I meant it."

"I know. And we did cool it. But like I said, I'm ready to start it up again."

I'm not, I thought. Logan had not understood at all.

The bracelet on my wrist felt as heavy as an iron chain.

CHAPTER 13

Saturday

Big news! What an exciting day. Mr. Prezzioso called this morning. He sounded frantic. And he had a right to sound that way. Mrs. P. was ready to go to the hospital to have the baby! Since it was an emergency sitting job, Mr. P. just started calling each of us BSC members, trying to find someone who could come stay with Jenny for the day. I was the first one he reached. And, oh, I just love babies!...

As you can tell, Jessi was ecstatic over her unexpected sitting job. Jenny is not one of her favorite sitting charges, but new babies *are* exciting, and besides, Mr. P. really did need someone to come over quickly.

So Jessi's Aunt Cecelia drove her to the Prezziosos'. Jessi knew that accepting this job without consulting Kristy or the other club members was okay. It was an emergency. Besides, Mr. P. had said over the phone, "Your friends are either out already, or their lines are busy."

"Well, I'm free," Jessi had told him. Two minutes later, she was sitting beside Cecelia in the front seat of her aunt's car.

Before she knew it, her aunt was pulling to a stop in front of the Prezziosos'.

" 'Bye, Aunt Cecelia!" Jessi called, as she scrambled out of the door. "I'll call when I hear any news. If I don't call, I'll be home by six. Mr. Prezzioso said that either he would come home then or, if he needed to stay at the hospital, Mrs. Frank from down the street will come spend the night with Jenny."

Aunt Cecelia smiled. "That's fine," she said. "I can't wait to hear the news." Jessi closed the door then, and her aunt drove slowly and carefully down the street, pausing once to let a squirrel cross the road.

Jessi, however, literally *sprinted* to Jenny's front door. She didn't even have to ring the bell. The door was flung open by Mr. P. Sitting nearby, on a bench in the hallway, was Mrs. P., a suitcase next to her. Both Mr. and Mrs. P. looked pretty tired. I guess you don't sleep well when you're expecting a baby.

"Where's Jenny?" was the first thing Jessi asked after she and the Prezziosos had hastily greeted one another.

"Still asleep," said Mrs. P., with a smile. "Jenny could sleep until noon every day, but we usually don't let her. However, we thought it would be okay today."

"So Jenny doesn't know you're leaving for the hospital?" asked Jessi, astounded. This did not seem like a very good situation to her.

"No," replied Mr. P., "but when she gets up, tell her I'll try to call her several times today. With any luck, one of the calls will be to say that the baby has arrived. But I'll call no matter what. We don't want Jenny to think we've abandoned her."

"Dear?" spoke up Mrs. P. "I really think we should leave now." She grimaced.

"Oh! Oh, right," exclaimed her husband,

sounding nervous again. He turned once more to Jessi. "You know where the emergency numbers are, you know where we'll be, and if you have any problems, Mrs. Frank will be home all day."

"Dear?" said Mrs. P. again.

With that, Mr. P. appeared to forget about Jessi. He helped his wife to her feet, picked up the suitcase, and walked her out the door, which Jessi held open for them. As they made their way slowly down the front walk, Mrs. P. leaned heavily on Mr. P. and Jessi had a sense of déjà vu. She remembered her old house in Oakley, New Jersey, she and Becca standing at *their* front door, their grandmother behind them, as all three watched Mr. Ramsey escort Mrs. Ramsey to the family car. Later that night, Squirt had been born.

Gosh, thought Jessi. That was about a year and a half ago. It could have been yesterday. And now Squirt was walking, climbing stairs. . . .

Jessi shook her head. The Prezziosos' car backed hurriedly down the driveway and into the street. Jessi watched until it was out of sight. Then she closed the front door and tiptoed up the stairs to Jenny's room. Her door was ajar, so Jessi peeked in. Jenny lay sprawled on her back, the covers kicked off, one arm slung over the side of the bed.

Jessi smiled, then tiptoed back downstairs. I'll fix Jenny a nice breakfast, she thought. Maybe that will take the sting out of waking up to find her parents gone — and her position as an only child about to come to an end.

Jessi had set the table, poured juice for Jenny, and was setting down bread and cereal, when Jenny shuffled into the kitchen.

"Morning, sleepyhead," teased Jessi. Then she added, "Do you remember who I am?" (She doesn't sit for Jenny very often.)

"Jessi?" said Jenny questioningly.

"That's right! You have a good memory."

"You're a baby-sitter," was Jenny's reply. She sounded as if she were accusing Jessi of committing a crime.

"That's right," said Jessi again.

"Then where are my mommy and daddy?"

"Why don't you sit down and have some breakfast," suggested Jessi. "I'll tell you everything while you're eating."

"Okay." Reluctantly, Jenny climbed onto her chair.

Jessi handed her a piece of toast and a bowl of cereal. Then she sat down across from Jenny. "Something wonderful happened this morning while you were asleep," she began, choosing her words carefully.

"What?" asked Jenny suspiciously.

"Your mommy decided she was ready to have the baby. So she and your daddy went to the hospital. Pretty soon you'll have a new brother or sister. Oh, and your daddy promised to call you today whenever he can. So you'll get to talk to him on the phone."

Jenny stopped eating her cereal, her spoon halfway to her mouth. She looked bewildered, then puzzled. Finally she said, "What about the stork?"

"The stork?" repeated Jessi. And then she remembered. She had read the BSC notebook and knew about Jenny's conversation with Stacey and Claud and me before Mrs. P.'s baby shower.

Uh-oh, thought Jessi. But she composed herself and said, "Jenny, storks don't bring babies. That's just a silly story. Babies grow inside of mommies."

Jenny looked quite thoughtful for several moments. She returned her spoon to her bowl. Then she opened her mouth (Jessi braced herself for the worst) and said, "I *thought* that stork thing sounded funny!"

And that was the end of the conversation. Jessi breathed a sigh of relief.

* * *

When breakfast was over, Jessi took Jenny upstairs to help her brush her teeth and get dressed. She let Jenny choose her own outfit (something she was pretty sure picky Mrs. P. never did). She figured it wouldn't matter. Mrs. P. would not see Jenny that day.

Jenny had just finished putting on her clothes — a pink jean skirt, a red shirt, yellow knee socks, and blue sandals — when the phone rang.

"Maybe it's Daddy!" Jenny shrieked. "Maybe my baby is here." (*Her* baby? wondered Jessi.) "Can I answer the phone? Please?"

"Do you know how to?" asked Jessi.

"Yes! Mommy taught me. It is a very grown-up thing to do. You can listen if you want." Jenny was already heading for the phone in her parents' bedroom.

"Okay," said Jessi. "Go to it."

Jenny snatched up the receiver. "Hello, Prezziosos'. Who's calling, please?" She listened for a moment. Then she said, "What? . . . What?" and then, "I have to ask." She took the phone away from her ear. "Jessi," she said, "the man wouldn't tell me his name.

But he wants to know if we want to buy some . . . cyclopediments?"

Jessi, suppressing a smile, said, "Tell him no, then say thank you and good-bye and hang up the phone."

Jenny did as she was told. Almost immediately the phone rang again. And Jenny snatched it up again. "Daddy!" she cried a moment later. "The stork story isn't true after all. Do I have a new baby yet?" She paused, then said, "Oh. Okay. Do you *promise* you'll call later? . . . Okay. 'Bye." Jenny sounded disappointed.

"Don't worry," said Jessi, confused because she thought Jenny didn't *want* the baby. "You'll have a new brother or sister by tonight. Or maybe tomorrow."

"Darn old baby," muttered Jenny, kicking at a chest of drawers. "I didn't know Mommy *and* Daddy would have to go away to get the baby. It'll never be just me and Mommy and Daddy again. The baby's got them all to itself right now. And I'll never have them to myself again."

Oh, thought Jessi. So *that* was why Jenny wanted the baby to come home soon. She didn't want it to have too much time alone with her parents. And she probably thought that if she took care of the baby as "hers," then Mr. and Mrs. P. would have more time to spend with Jenny.

It was very complicated.

Jessi managed to entertain Jenny for the rest of the morning. She made a few phone calls to let some of the other BSC members know what was going on. She gave Jenny lunch.

Jenny was just finishing her peanut butter sandwich when the phone rang again. Jenny made a leap for it. "I hope it's my daddy!" she cried.

It was, but he didn't have any news. No baby yet.

Jenny was becoming edgy. And cranky.

"How about a nap?" asked Jessi tiredly.

"NO!"

"Okay, okay."

At 4:15, the phone rang again. "You get it this time," said Jenny, who was slumped in a chair, the picture of depression.

So Jessi did. And it was Mr. P. "The baby's here!" he said excitedly. "It's a girl, she weighs seven and a half pounds, and she's twenty-one inches long. Her name is Andrea."

"Congratulations!" shouted Jessi. "Wait, let me put Jenny on the phone."

Jenny listened to her father with absolutely no expression on her face. Then she said good-bye and slumped back into her chair.

Jessi barely noticed. She called her family and every single club member, including Logan and Shannon, to spread the news. When she finally got off the phone, she said excitedly to Jenny, "So what do you think? You have a baby sister."

Jenny narrowed her eyes. "I wanted a brother," she said, and marched up to her room.

Jessi watched her helplessly.

Mrs. Prezzioso and Andrea stayed in the hospital for three days. On Tuesday afternoon, Mr. P. was allowed to bring them home. The day before, he had called during the BSC meeting to line up a sitter for Jenny for the afternoon. I had gotten the job.

When I rang the Prezziosos' bell on Tuesday, I was greeted by Mrs. Frank, who had been staying with Jenny since the night before. I had a feeling that Jenny's life since Saturday had consisted of a string of baby-sitters. I also had a feeling that Jenny was not going to be in a good mood. I was right about both things.

I said good-bye to Mrs. Frank and let her out the front door. Then I walked into the living room, where Jenny and Mrs. Frank had obviously been reading books.

"Hey, Jen," I greeted her. "Andrea comes home today!" I sounded as perky and as excited as I was able.

"So?" countered Jenny.

"Well, today *is* sort of important. You're a big sister and your baby sister is coming home."

Jenny didn't answer me.

"Your dad's going to drive everyone home in an hour or so."

"Yup." Jenny finally looked up from her copy of *The Little Engine That Could*. "And I will never have Mommy and Daddy all to myself again."

"Oh, Jen." I sat on the floor beside her. "That's not true. Mommies and daddies have time for more than one child. Think about Mal's family."

"I know." (Jenny heaved a sigh that was probably heard in China.) "But it won't be the same."

"No. You're right. It won't be the same. I bet your mom and dad will make special time just for you, though."

"Maybe."

"You know what?" I said. "My mom died when I was little, so I grew up without brothers or sisters. It was just my dad and me. And sometimes I was really lonely. I wished and wished for a brother or sister. Especially a *baby* brother or sister. I wanted to have someone to take care of."

122

"You did?"

"Yup. Anyway, then my dad married Dawn's mom, so now Dawn is my sister. She's not a baby sister to take care of, and every now and then we fight, but mostly we're glad to have each other. Sometimes at night when we're supposed to be in bed, one of us will sneak into the other's room and we'll stay up late, talking and talking in the dark."

"That sounds like fun," said Jenny . . . uncertainly.

"What's the matter?" I asked her.

"Babies seem like a lot of work. And Mommy wants me to be a big girl now. She wants me to do grown-up, big-girl things."

"But you'll still be your mommy's little girl. Nothing will change that."

"Yes it will!" Jenny shouted suddenly, startling me. "Andrea will change everything. I'll have to give her bottles the way I practiced on that darn old doll, and I'll have to — "

"Whoa, Jenny. Calm down," I told her. "You won't know how things will be with Andrea until you actually see her." Jenny got up and stomped around the living room. "Okay, kiddo," I said. "Outdoors."

"Why?"

"Because you have a lot of energy to get rid

of, and I'm going to teach you a new game. It's really fun and funny."

"What is it?" asked Jenny suspiciously.

"It's called Flamingo Fight."

Jenny giggled. "Okay," she said.

So we put on our jackets and mittens and went outside. Luckily the snow that had fallen had long since melted, and the grass was dry. (You need a soft, dry outdoor place that's not too near the street to play Flamingo Fight, because you fall down a lot.)

"Oh, wait," I said to Jenny as soon as we were outdoors. "I've got to get us blindfolds. You sit right here on the front steps and don't move. I'll be back in just a second."

I dashed inside, grabbed two woolen scarves from the Prezziosos' closet, and dashed back out. Jenny was sitting where I'd left her.

"Okay. First thing," I began. "Do you know what a flamingo is?"

Smiling, Jenny got up. Then she tried to balance on one leg.

"That's right!" I said. "A flamingo is a bird that stands on only one of its legs. It tucks the other one up under its body. You can pretend to be a flamingo by bending your leg up behind you and holding your foot with your hand. Then you can hop around on your other leg."

"Okay," said Jenny, trying it. "But what about the fight?"

"Well, what you do in a flamingo fight is try to make the other person fall down. If you can do that, you win. But there are some rules. You have to tie a scarf around your face so that you can't see. Then, we call out to each other so that I know where you are, and you know where I am. We try to bump into each other. If I make you fall down, I'm the winner. If you make me fall down, you're the winner. One important thing, though. We can't use our hands. We just hop and bump around in the darkness."

Jenny was laughing by then. "Let's play!" she cried.

So I tied a scarf around Jenny's eyes (I was careful not to cover her nose) and made sure she couldn't see. Then I tied a scarf around my eyes. "Jen?" I said.

"Yeah. I'm here."

"Are you holding one foot up?"

"Yup."

"Okay. Then get ready to . . . flamingo fight!"

I hopped in the direction in which I'd heard Jenny say, "Yup." But I didn't run into anything. "Jen?" I called. I heard giggling from the opposite direction, turned around, and hopped toward the sound. Suddenly I bumped into Jenny. "Flamingo fight!" I cried.

Laughing, Jenny and I kept bumping into each other, until finally I lost my balance and fell down.

"You win!" I said. "The score is one to nothing, in favor of you."

"Yea!" shouted Jenny.

Twenty minutes later, the game was tied five to five, and Jenny and I were desperately trying to knock each other over, when we heard the honking of a car.

"I think that's Mommy and Daddy . . . and Andrea!" exclaimed Jenny. In her excitement, she rushed toward the driveway, ran into me, and knocked me to the ground.

"Hey, you win!" I told Jenny, slipping the scarf from over my eyes.

Then, "Jen, wait!" I called, realizing that Jenny was tearing toward the driveway blindfolded. I caught up with her and removed *her* scarf. The two of us stood at the edge of the driveway and watched Mr. P. park the car.

He pulled gently to a stop by the front walk, got out of the car, and hurried around to Mrs. P's door. Then he took the baby from her, and Mrs. P. climbed slowly out of the car herself. She knelt down and held her arms open wide. "Jenny!" she said. "I missed you."

Jenny flew toward her mother, and I thought, Oh, what a nice reunion.

But at the last moment, Jenny veered to the side, stood on tiptoe in front of her father, and said, "Let me see Andrea."

I couldn't tell whether Mrs. P. looked hurt or relieved or proud or all three things at once. At any rate, she and I both watched as Mr. P. bent down, cradling the baby, and Jenny got her first look at her sister.

Andrea was wrapped up in blankets. Only her face and her tiny hands showed. She was wide awake and she looked as if she were staring solemnly at her sister, who stared back at her.

For a few moments, Jenny and Andrea continued to stare at each other. Then Andrea's hands moved slightly and Jenny held out a tentative finger. She touched one hand. She leaned over for a closer look.

"She has fingernails!" said Jenny softly. "She has real fingernails, but they're so *little*." She paused and said, "Ooh, Andrea is *much* better than my doll. Can I hold her, Daddy?"

"When we're inside," replied Mr. P. "And before we go in, why don't you give your mom a big hug? She missed you."

"I missed you, too, Mommy," said Jenny, as everyone stood up. "I'm glad you came back." She hugged Mrs. P. around the legs.

Jenny took her mother's hand and they followed Mr. P. and Andrea inside. *I* followed Jenny and her mother.

The first thing Jenny said when we were indoors was, "Can I hold the baby now?"

"Let's take off our coats first," replied her mother.

So we did. A few minutes later, Jenny was sitting in an armchair, her feet sticking out in front of her, and Mr. P. and I were watching as Jenny's mother placed Andrea in her sister's waiting arms.

I hope that the Prezziosos saw what I saw then: As Jenny looked down at her new sister, and gently stroked a hand, an arm, a cheek, her entire face changed.

I could tell it was love at first sight.

Jenny loved Andrea, her new sister.

Oh, sure, there would be tough times ahead for them. They would quarrel, fight, slam doors, not speak to each other, go on car trips and divide the backseat in half so that neither sister touched the other's belongings. Just like Dawn and me. We fight sometimes. But mostly we're good friends. We stick up for each other and we have fun together.

I could tell that that was the way things would be for Jenny and Andrea, too.

Jenny bent over. She and Andrea were nose to nose. "Hello, Andrea," said Jenny. "I'm your big sister. I know you can't do many things yet, so I will help you. Maybe when you're three or four I'll teach you how to play Flamingo Fight. I'll be seven or eight by then. I'll be going to school and you won't, so I'll tell you all about school."

Jenny stopped talking. She stroked the black downy hair on Andrea's head. "Don't worry, Mommy," said Jenny, looking up. "I remember about the soft spot. I won't hurt the baby."

By that time, the Prezziosos were filming this scene on their camcorder. But Mrs. P. stopped watching her daughters long enough to pay me. Then I went home.

CHAPTER 15

Wow.

Did I ever do some heavy thinking as I walked from Jenny's house to mine.

I was thinking about relationships. I thought about Dawn and me, and what good friends we are. Even when we fight, we learn something from our fights. We learn how to listen to each other and respect each other.

I was thinking about Jenny and Andrea. In my wildest dreams I had never imagined that Andrea's homecoming would have worked out the way it had. Not with the conversations the BSC members had been having with Jenny. Not with Jenny throwing her doll around her room. Not with Jenny's fears about no longer being her parents' "one and only."

I suppose that sometimes some family members *never* get along, but I don't think that happens often. Usually when people are mad, some sort of love is underlying the feelings that show, the feelings on the outside. When people love each other — whether they're brothers and sisters, parents and children, best friends, husbands and wives, or girlfriends and boyfriends — that love leads to an understanding. That's why I can (usually) ignore my father when he gets into one of his orderliness frenzies. It's why my stepmother doesn't force me to eat the foods (such as tofu) that she and Dawn adore. And it's why Dawn and I can fight and make up.

Then I thought about Logan and me. What did this say about us? I had tried to be understanding of Logan, but was he understanding of me? He used to be, that's for sure. I remembered my thirteenth birthday. There had been a surprise party. Since I'm shy, you can imagine how I felt about being surprised with a cake and gifts. I *hated* being the center of attention. Being the center of attention is right up there with performing and public speaking. I'm terrified of those things. And when I ran out on my own party that evening, Logan understood. He gave me a chance to get myself together. Then we talked about things, and Logan never made me the center of attention again, if he could possibly help it. He didn't mind when I'd agree to go to a school dance — and then not dance. He let me make up my mind about going to Hallow- een parties in costumes or in regular clothes. . . . He *used* to be that way.

Now he wasn't.

I felt that he didn't listen to me anymore. He thought only about what *he* wanted, while I tried to understand him and what he wanted, and to make allowances for him. Not that he would have forced me to dance at a school hop — or would he have? I wasn't sure. What I *was* sure about, though, was that he expected me to be available for him at all times. He seemed to have forgotten that I had a family and another life, and that they did not include Logan.

Logan wanted me to be "Logan's girl," and I didn't want to be anybody's girl. Ever. I may not be as independent as my sister, but I have rights and feelings like anyone else.

I did not want to be owned.

By the time I reached our house, I had made a decision.

First, I went to my room. I opened my jew- elry box, removed something from it, and slipped it into my pocket.

Then I telephoned Logan.

"Hi," I said when he picked up the phone. "It's me."

"Hi, you!"

"Logan, I have to talk to you. Now. Can we meet in the park?"

"It's late, Mary Anne. It's getting dark out. Why do you have to meet me somewhere? Can't we just talk? Or can't we see each other in school tomorrow? I'm not — "

"No," I interrupted.

"Mary *Anne*."

"Logan, when *you* call *me* on the spur of the moment and want me to go out, I usually do it. Now I'm asking you to do the same thing for me." I paused. Then I went on, "We'll meet at the bench by the skating pond."

"Oh, okay! Remember that snowy afternoon in the park? That was great, wasn't it?"

"Yeah. But Logan, you don't need to bring your skates. I can't stay out very long."

"Me, neither," replied Logan agreeably. "See you in a few minutes."

We hung up the phone.

"Dawn!" I called. (She was in her room, studying.) "I'm going to meet Logan in the park now."

"*Now?*"

"Yeah. I know it's late, but I only have to

see him for a few minutes. I'll be back before six o'clock."

"You shouldn't let Logan push you around like this," was Dawn's reply.

I almost told her that *I* was doing the pushing, but I didn't have time. Besides, by this evening I'd probably have a lot more to tell her, so I just yelled, "Later!" Then I put on my parka and mittens and ran out the door and all the way to the park.

The park looked very different than it had a few weeks earlier. The snow was gone. Scrubby brown grass showed in its place. The tree branches were bare, dark against the late afternoon sky. No snow outlined them, turning them into fairy trees. Only a few people were still enjoying the park; the children had left.

And yet just *seeing* the park brought back all sorts of memories. It brought back good times that Logan and I had shared there. And those memories led to other memories.

I pictured Logan and me wearing cat costumes to the Halloween Hop.

I pictured us on a joint baby-sitting job for Jackie Rodowsky. That was before Logan and I were boyfriend and girlfriend.

I remembered the first time I had spotted Logan in school, when he was the new boy —

and I couldn't take my eyes off of him.

I could not believe what I was going to do.

When I reached the bench it was empty.

I sat down and waited.

Logan was not likely to be late.

And he wasn't. I'd been sitting alone for less than a minute when I heard him call, "Hi, Mary Anne!"

He was loping toward me, jogging through the park. Smiling.

Oh, I thought. What am I doing? What am I going to do to Logan? What am I going to do to us?

But my mind was made up.

Logan sank down next to me. He tilted my chin toward him so we could kiss, but I pulled away.

"What's wrong?" asked Logan. "Here we are in the park. Don't — "

I put my hand over Logan's mouth to make him stop talking. It was Logan's turn to pull away. But then he leaned toward me and tried to kiss me again. Why wasn't he getting the message?

Oh.

Because I wasn't talking. I thought my actions were enough, but maybe not. After all, Logan couldn't read my thoughts.

"Logan . . . Logan?" I began.

"Yes? Yes?" Logan laughed at his joke.

"Logan, this is serious," I said. (Logan's smile vanished.) "Remember how I said we needed to cool our relationship?"

"Of course," answered Logan. "And we did."

"No. *I* did. You never took it seriously."

"I did too!" exclaimed Logan indignantly.

"But then you decided to start things up again, without asking me."

"I don't have to ask your permission for everything."

"No, but you need to listen to me. And understand me. I don't feel like you do either of those things anymore. You haven't for a long time." I could feel my hands growing clammy in my mittens, but I was determined to say what I'd planned to say. "I was the one who asked to cool our relationship for awhile, and you agreed. Don't you think it would have been courteous to consult me when you felt we were ready to start seeing more of each other?"

"Courteous?" repeated Logan. "Who are you? Miss Manners?"

"No, I'm Mary Anne Spier and I am a person. An independent person who likes to think for herself and have some freedom." (I

136

was shaking; wondering just how independent I was — or wanted to be.)

"What exactly are you saying, Mary Anne?"

"I want to break up with you," I replied. I didn't even hesitate before I said it.

"You *what?*"

"I want to break up with you. It's time to do that. This relationship isn't going anywhere. I don't know about you, but I'm not happy."

"Mary Anne — "

Logan stopped talking when I stood up, took off one mitten, and reached into my pocket. From it, I pulled the heart bracelet that Logan had given me on Valentine's Day. Then I reached for Logan's hand, dropped the bracelet into it, and closed his fingers around the linked hearts.

"I can't keep this," I told him.

"You're serious, aren't you?" said Logan.

"Yes," I replied softly.

Logan opened his hand. He looked at the bracelet coiled in it. Then he looked back at me. "I guess this means we're — we're not — " Logan had to stop speaking because his voice had choked up. (I was choked up, too.)

"Good-bye, Logan," I said.

"Good-bye, Mary Anne."

About the Author

ANN M. MARTIN did *a lot* of baby-sitting when she was growing up in Princeton, New Jersey. Now her favorite baby-sitting charge is her cat, Mouse, who lives with her in her Manhattan apartment.

Ann Martin's Apple Paperbacks include *Yours Turly, Shirley; Ten Kids, No Pets; With You and Without You; Bummer Summer;* and all the other books in the Baby-sitters Club series.

She is a former editor of books for children, and was graduated from Smith College. She likes ice cream, the beach, and *I Love Lucy;* and she hates to cook.

Look for #42

JESSI AND THE
DANCE SCHOOL PHANTOM

After rehearsal, I collapsed onto the bench in the dressing room as I pulled out my dance bag. I felt tired, but in a good way — and I felt satisfied with my dancing that day. I took my hair out of its ponytail and shook it out. Then I reached into my dance bag and I knew right away that something was wrong.

My jeans and my shirt were still in there, and so were my sneakers. But my whole spare outfit was gone. No black leotard, no pink tights. No leg warmers (I'd worn the white ones, so it was the purple ones that were missing) and no sweat shirt. No spare toe shoes.

"Oh, my lord," I said, under my breath. (That's one of Claudia's favorite expressions, and we've all picked it up.) I looked around to see if anyone was noticing *me* noticing my empty bag. They were all busy with their own stuff.

I shrugged. What was I going to do about it? There was a thief in our midst (as they would say in a Nancy Drew book) but I wasn't going to catch her that night. I was too exhausted to even think about it.

I pulled on my school clothes and bent over to put on my shoes. Then I saw it. Once again, a note was tucked into the laces of my left sneaker. Only this time, the note was written in blood!

I gasped. Oh, how creepy. Hiding my toe shoes was no big deal. Stealing my extra dance clothes was worse, but it still wasn't a federal offense. But a note written in blood! Ew. For a minute I thought I was going to pass out.

Then I looked closer and saw that it wasn't blood at all. It was just red ink. But this time, it didn't say BEWARE. This time, it said this: WATCH YOUR STEP. As I read it, I shivered. Then I crumpled it up and stuck it into my bag. This was getting a little too scary. Somebody was really out to get me. But why?

**Read all the books
in the Baby-sitters Club series
by Ann M. Martin**

Super Specials:

1 *Baby-sitters on Board!*
   Guess who's going on a dream vacation? The Baby-sitters!

2 *Baby-sitters' Summer Vacation*
   Good-bye, Stoneybrook . . . hello, Camp Mohawk!

3 *Baby-sitters' Winter Vacation*
   The Baby-sitters are off for a week of winter fun!

4 *Baby-sitters' Island Adventure*
   Two of the Baby-sitters are shipwrecked!

5 *California Girls!*
   A winning lottery ticket sends the Baby-sitters to *California!*

THE BABY-SITTERS CLUB®

by Ann M. Martin

The Baby-sitters' business is booming! And that gets Stacey, Kristy, Claudia, and the rest of The Baby-sitters Club members in all kinds of adventures...at school, with boys, and, of course, baby-sitting!

Something new and exciting happens in every Baby-sitters Club book.
Collect and read them all!

More titles... ▶

The Baby-sitters Club titles continued...

❏	MG42501-3	#28	Welcome Back, Stacey!	$2.95
❏	MG42500-5	#29	Mallory and the Mystery Diary	$2.95
❏	MG42498-X	#30	Mary Anne and the Great Romance	$2.95
❏	MG42497-1	#31	Dawn's Wicked Stepsister	$2.95
❏	MG42496-3	#32	Kristy and the Secret of Susan	$2.95
❏	MG42495-5	#33	Claudia and the Great Search	$2.95
❏	MG42494-7	#34	Mary Anne and Too Many Boys	$2.95
❏	MG42508-0	#35	Stacey and the Mystery of Stoneybrook	$2.95
❏	MG43565-5	#36	Jessi's Baby-sitter	$2.95
❏	MG43566-3	#37	Dawn and the Older Boy	$2.95
❏	MG43567-1	#38	Kristy's Mystery Admirer	$2.95
❏	MG43568-X	#39	Poor Mallory!	$2.95
❏	MG43569-8	#40	Claudia and the Middle School Mystery (Jan. '91)	$2.95
❏	MG43570-1	#41	Mary Anne Versus Logan (Feb. '91)	$2.95
❏	MG44240-6		Baby-sitters on Board! Super Special #1	$3.50
❏	MG44239-2		Baby-sitters' Summer Vacation Super Special #2	$3.50
❏	MG43973-1		Baby-sitters' Winter Vacation Super Special #3	$3.50
❏	MG42493-9		Baby-sitters' Island Adventure Super Special #4	$3.50
❏	MG43575-2		California Girls! Super Special #5	$3.50
❏	MG43745-3		The Baby-sitters Club 1990-91 Student Planner and Date Book	$7.95
❏	MG43744-5		The Baby-sitters Club 1991 Calendar	$8.95
❏	MG43803-4		The Baby-sitters Club Notebook	$1.95

Available wherever you buy books...or use this order form.

Scholastic Inc., P.O. Box 7502, 2931 E. McCarty Street, Jefferson City, MO 65102

Please send me the books I have checked above. I am enclosing $_____
(please add $2.00 to cover shipping and handling). Send check or money order — no cash or C.O.D.s please.

Name _____

Address _____

City _____ State/Zip _____

Please allow four to six weeks for delivery. Offer good in the U.S. only. Sorry, mail orders are not available to residents of Canada. Prices subject to change.

Have fun in the sun with your new

THE BABY-SITTERS CLUB®

Beach Towel!

200 Winners

Enter THE BABY-SITTERS CLUB FUN IN THE SUN GIVEAWAY!

Win a really cool beach towel! It's giant-sized, 100% cotton, and has the official Baby-sitters Club logo on it! Just fill in the coupon below and return it by March 31, 1991.

The Baby-sitters Club Fun in the Sun Giveaway

Name _____ Age _____

Street _____

City _____ State _____ Zip _____

Where did you buy this *Baby-sitters Club* book?

☐ Bookstore   ☐ Drugstore   ☐ Supermarket   ☐ Library
☐ Book Club   ☐ Book Fair   ☐ Other_____ (specify)   BSC690